Pain . . . . ssion

As Marianne arrived at the shed she could hear someone humming a tune inside. Then there was a crash, and a curse singed the air.

She looked inside to see if someone needed her assistance. The only man there was Sherry, and another curse erupted from his lips as he stared at his bloodied thumb. He stared at her, and she stared at him as the revelation dawned. He didn't know how to use a hammer. Before she could make clear her observation to him, he'd taken two steps toward her, his arms held wide. With a question in his eyes, he swept her into his embrace. She swayed with shock as he pressed a very hot and demanding kiss to her lips. . . .

Diamond Books by Maria Greene

DARING GAMBLE
LOVER'S KNOT
GENTLEMAN BUTLER

Gentleman Butler

Maria Greene

DIAMOND BOOKS, NEW YORK

This book is a Diamond original edition,
and has never been previously published.

GENTLEMAN BUTLER

A Diamond Book / published by arrangement with
the author

PRINTING HISTORY
Diamond edition / April 1993

ISBN: 1-55773-888-2

Diamond Books are published by The Berkley Publishing Group,
200 Madison Avenue, New York, NY 10016.
The name "DIAMOND" and its logo
are trademarks belonging to Charter Communications, Inc.

PRINTED IN THE UNITED STATES OF AMERICA

10   9   8   7   6   5   4   3   2   1

Gentleman
Butler

Chapter One

"LEITH, THESE LETTERS WILL BE THE END OF ME! I can't conceive of anyone who would write such a dastardly accusation," the Dowager Lady Longford said to the Honorable Leith Sheridan, her grandson, and waved a stack of papers in her hand. "Forcing an old woman to comply with extortion. Bah! 'Twill be the end of me. I have paid out two thousand pounds already, and the villain wants more." She crushed the letters between her frail hands and tossed them on to her escritoire. Her eyes softening, she glanced at Leith from under imperious gray eyebrows. "Kind of you to offer to look into the matter."

"Most likely the perpetrator is related in some way to Lord Randome. How else could your—ahem—daring love epistles to the old earl have come to light when he died?" Leith fixed his grandparent with a probing stare. "The relatives must have sorted through his documents. The culprit is Mordecay Follett, Randome's nephew, I'll warrant. He always has pockets to let."

"Horrible thought that someone we know would be so

1

callous as to extort money from me, Leith. There's the frightful possibility that the letters might come under public scrutiny one day. A scandal 'twould be for sure.'' The old lady fluttered her hands in front of her face as if finding the room too hot.

It *was* hot, Leith thought. A fire burned, although the month of May was well under way. Grandmother daily complained about her cold bones and always kept a fire in the grate. Leith gently inserted a long finger under his starched collar to allow for some ventilation. ''I must say I was appalled at the insinuation that Father might have been Randome's by-blow. That piece of nonsense could bring ruin to our family.''

The Dowager Lady Longford gave him a scornful glance. ''I assure you, th' accusation is flummery. I'll allow I was a high-spirited girl fifty years ago, and I admit it was wholly unacceptable of me to write secret epistles to a gentleman—but—I was in love. However, the affair never went further than the exchanging of a few clandestine missives.'' Delicate color tinted the dowager's sunken cheeks, and she fidgeted with the eyeglass ribbon around her neck. ''I'll allow the contents were somewhat wicked, but, as I said before, love played a great role. I'm not sure you know the exhilaration of being in love, Leith. I suspect you're too mercurial of spirit for a lasting emotion. Even though you're betrothed to Vivian Worton, you are an incorrigible flirt. Perhaps you always will be, but you can't delay your wedding much longer.''

Leith gave her his grin, which—he'd found out countless times—never failed to charm. ''What's the hurry? I'll wait until I'm forty to set up my nursery.''

''Forty?'' the dowager snorted. ''You're about in your head, Leith. Vivian certainly won't wait that long.

Anyway, no one will have you once you've developed a paunch and a pink shiny pate, and lost the starch in your muscles.''

''It was Father who wanted me to marry Vivian.''

''When Vivian's father died, your father promised that he would look after her.''

Leith sighed. ''And he tied her to me. Certainly not a match made in heaven, but I will obey Father's wishes.''

The dowager studied her beloved grandson. The young ladies of polite society were always dimpling and blushing in his presence, and the dowager knew he had crushed many a tender heart. Not that he was calculating and heartless; he was volatile, always had been.

Had he ever truly loved? She doubted it. She surveyed his coat of Bath superfine, the perfect folds of his neckcloth, and the highly polished Hessians. Elegant as always, she observed. Leith could boast of a handsome face, a tall, athletic body, and broad shoulders—not to mention that devastating grin. He's so like old Longford, Lady Antonia thought as the memory of her long-dead husband came to mind—even down to the dent in his stubborn chin. The chestnut hair that waved gently over a high brow, the straight dark bar of eyebrows, the slightly hooked nose were all Longford features. However, the mischievous gleam in his blue eyes and the easy grace came from his mother's side of the family.

Lady Lindell Longford had been a veritable butterfly, a wisp of gracefulness without a single serious thought in her head. Thank God young Leith had inherited the Longford common sense. His elder brother, John, the current Baron Longford, had too much of the Longford stodginess, and none of his brother's charm. Leith was her favorite grandchild, she thought with a sigh. But John, his wife, and their brood of children would have to be protected against any hint of scandal. Leith was the only relative she could trust in this horrid predicament. He always understood her, read her thoughts with uncanny accuracy, and never berated her for her small eccentricities—as John always did. Leith was a perfect gentleman, the kindest of souls, and she wished he would find a woman—other than Vivian—to match his lively spirit one day. Not that she would voice such a scandalous thought. She was pleased that he'd been forced to sell out from the army after a chest wound he'd received at one of the battles in the Peninsular war. He was healed now, but one of his lungs would always remain weaker than the other. Not that it seemed to bother him in the slightest.

"Why did you marry Longford if you loved Lord Randome?" her grandson asked shrewdly. "You ought to have wed him."

"Marry Randome?" Her eyes widened in surprise. "I couldn't very well go against my parents' wishes. I was promised to Longford since my birth."

Leith's lips twitched. "Why did you let that stop you?" With a warm feeling of affection, he watched his grandmama. The formidable dowager looked deceptively fragile with her dainty features and flyaway white hair. The back was still as straight as a ruler, the tilt of her chin proud, and the eyes wise. Not much passed unnoticed before those faded blue eyes, he thought, and remembered the days of his childhood when Lady Antonia had upbraided him for mischief. However severe a disciplinarian, she had also been his staunchest support, and best friend. When his parents died in a coaching accident, she had stood by him in his grief, and now she needed his help. "Well? What stopped you?" he repeated.

"Randome was betrothed to another woman. A more

totty-headed female than Lady Eudora Randome you cannot find on the face of this earth.'' Another sigh quivered on the dowager's lips. ''Randome showed a shocking lack of taste when he chose her.''

''If you had married him, you might have made a terrible mistake,'' Leith went on mercilessly. ''I think Randome was rather a bully and a bore. A rake and an inveterate gamester.'' Leith was taking tea with his grandmother and gingerly sipped from the gilded edge of a fine bone-china cup. He eyed the cucumber sandwiches suspiciously, knowing full well the bread would be stale and the cucumber limp.

''You're rapier-sharp as usual, Leith,'' she observed. ''Randome wasn't like that in his youth, but you didn't know him then. Besides, being married to Lady Randome must have taken the spirit out of him.''

''I agree she's a wet blanket, but *age* might have done that to her.'' As he winked the dowager gave him a scathing glance.

''Age? Has nothing to do with it.'' However much she tried to maintain a mask of disapproval, mischief glittered in her eyes. ''I don't know from whom you learned such disrespect for your elders.''

Leith gave a wide smile. ''Mayhap from you, Grandmama.''

Her face darkened, but soon the thin shoulders heaved in a chuckle. ''You rapscallion!''

The old dowager looked a fright in her black bombazine gown, red sequined slippers, and yellow-and-purple-striped wool muffler wound around her neck three times. A cluster of false grapes nestled in her hair, which was, as always, escaping the bun at the nape, and a garish baroque spray of rubies was pinned to her bodice.

"Let me hear, what are your plans for the dratted letters?" she asked, and crumbled a piece of marble cake on her plate with a fork. She dipped a cube into the tea before popping it into her mouth. "Randome's corpse isn't in London any longer."

"I suppose I'd better go down to Kent and snoop around Randome's Folly. What's the name of the village anyway? It has slipped my mind."

"Spiggott Hollow," Lady Antonia said with a snort. "With a name like that, the village is bound to be filled with imbeciles."

"I'm inclined to agree with you there," Leith said dryly. "The place will be as dull as ditch water." He paused and rubbed his chin in thought. "What I don't understand is why a cold cod like Randome would have kept your love letters all this time."

"I told you, he wasn't always a cold fish." She hummed as if thinking hard, then said, "What if they recognize you in Spiggott Hollow? If the extortionist is there for the funeral, he—or she—might suspect your errand in Kent. It isn't as if we have a reason to be in the vicinity of Randome's Folly, since we have no relation there." She straightened her ruby brooch. "Don't you have some friends you could visit in Kent, Leith?"

He shook his head. "They are all here in London for the season. Won't return to the country until midsummer. What excuse shall I invent for leaving London during the season?"

The dowager pondered his question while chewing vigorously. The only sounds in the room were the tall clock ticking in the corner and the crackling fire. Leith could remember that special *tick-tock* since infancy, and the sound added to the cheerful atmosphere of home. His gaze wandered leisurely around the parlor of the old town house on Upper Brook Street. The house had belonged to the Longfords for three generations, and those generations had furnished it until every room was crammed with a hodgepodge of styles. Every surface was filled with knick-knacks, and most of the faded brocade-paneled walls were covered with old portraits. Lady Antonia fit into the paraphernalia like a well-worn favorite chair.

"I have the perfect solution," the dowager cried, her face alight with mischief. "You must seek employment at Spiggott Hollow, preferably at the Folly, and thus be free to snoop around until you discover the truth."

Leith laughed. "You never lost your sense for the ridiculous, Grandmama."

"You must admit 'tis a great scheme, Leith." She pursed her lips in thought. "You know everything there's to know about horses. You're exceptionally strong, and you have a great flair for dancing. Besides, you paint watercolors tolerably well."

"Outstanding recommendations," he said dryly.

Aflutter with excitement, she rose from her chair and took a step toward him. "You could lend your skills as a stable groom or seek a painting instructor post at the Folley."

Leith's eyes widening in amazement, he said, "That's preposterous, Grandmama. Without a disguise, I'll be recognized on my first day there."

The dowager pooh-poohed. "Don't be negative. A disguise will be just the thing. We must create one today."

"Really, Grandmama! 'Tis the most idiotic idea you've ever expressed. I would have to pay attendance to Randome's widow and her retinue." He gave a shudder and half rose out of his chair, but the dowager pushed him back down.

"You promised to help me, Leith. You can do anything you set your mind to." The old woman swept the ends of her striped woolen muffler back over her shoulders. "All we have to do is put our minds together and form a plan."

Leith leaned back uneasily. The carving in the high back of the chair gnawed into his shoulder blades. "It isn't as easy as you think to don a whole new personality and fool a whole village of people."

"Pshaw! Where's your spirit of adventure? Anyhow, the Longfords never mixed with the Randomes. They won't know you." The dowager leaned over him, her eyes gleaming. The odor of camphor wafted toward him. Camphor was his grandmother's cure-all. Every morning she had two drops on a lump of sugar.

"What about my voice? My accent will be different. The villagers will know I'm not one of them." Leith thought for a moment. His sense for the ridiculous was tickled, yet he feared his grandmother's next words.

"Then you'll have to contort it during the time it takes to discover the person who means to pull the Longford name through the mud. You'll have to do this for the family honor, Leith."

"Contort?" Leith said weakly, knowing full well there was no stopping his mischief-loving grandmother now. "I should certainly hope not!"

Three days later

In an urn, Miss Marianne Darby arranged the bouquet of red and yellow tulips she had carried to her mother's grave at the graveyard of St. Mary's in the center of Spiggott Hollow. A willow wren warbled in the tree branch above, and sadness tugged at Marianne's heart.

Three years had passed since her mother's death, but the loneliness still hurt. Mother had been her greatest friend, and Marianne had difficulty finding something in Spiggott Hollow to fill the void her parent had left behind.

Father was there for her, of course, but her relationship with him was different. Squire Darby was the hearty type who loved horses above any human being; he loved the hunt, the races, and the breeding of purebloods.

Marianne like horses very well, but she also had other interests, like reading and attending musicales. Her father had no interest in the more subtle pleasures of life, nor did her chaperon, Miss Dew. Her mother had shared those amusements. The squire was a strict man, a stickler for propriety who always demanded a detailed account of Marianne's day every evening at supper. In his youth he'd been an ardent member of a pugilist society, and he wasn't above cuffing a disobedient servant. She sensed that he loved her despite his strict views, and always listened to her opinions.

Marianne sighed as she thought about her father. She could set the clocks at her house after his habits, that's how regular they were. He would never change his ways, not even for one hour of the day. But she had no real complaint. He ran the prosperous Darby household to perfection, and Marianne lacked no creature comforts in her life.

For that reason, she could concentrate on helping others. She smiled as she contemplated the flower arrangement. According to Miss Dew, she lent her considerable energy, deductive powers, and great organizational skills to managing her friends' lives at Spiggott Hollow. ''Somewhat of an exaggeration,'' Marianne said to herself, yet she could not deny that she took a lively interest in the village matters.

"Julia Wellesly wouldn't be betrothed today unless I had pushed her into Gregory's arms," she continued with a sigh of contentment as she remembered her best friend, the "poor relation" of the Randomes. Julia would have ended up on the shelf like herself if Marianne hadn't organized Julia's coming-out ball at Darby House. And her cousin, Gregory Allister, was a good friend as well. A pity he was away, fighting for his country in the Peninsular war. "I wish Father wouldn't go on about another season in London," Marianne whispered to her mother's ghost as yet another wren joined his mate in the tree. "It was humiliating not to *take,* and I don't want to go through that again."

Warm breezes and sunlight wafted around her, as if eager to dispel the sudden dark cloud in her mind. She would not go to London to be ridiculed again. No man in his right mind would marry a woman who wasn't physically flawless, except the tedious Swinton Langley, perhaps, but then she would never accept his offer. Death would be preferable.

She touched her stiff hip self-consciously, wondering if she would have been married by now if she hadn't fallen down the hayloft ladder twenty years ago and broken her hip. Maybe, maybe not. It was no use speculating. She would like to raise a family before it was too late, but that dream she tucked away hastily every time it emerged in her mind.

She pulled some weeds from the flower border around the grave and rubbed a spot of moss from the marble headstone. "Father is very obstinate at times, Mama. He goes on and on about another London season, says I should visit Aunt Netta. He wants to get me off his hands." She traced the lettering on the stone. "But as you well know, I'm more stubborn than Father. He'll give up this harebrained notion soon enough." Somehow the words rang hollow, and Marianne sighed. Rising, she brushed the dust from her dress and looked through the dappled sunlight toward the church.

On the raked gravel in front of the church steps, she saw a tall stranger staring up at the pointed spire. She had heard that the latest arrival in Spiggott Hollow was the new Randome butler. Perhaps this gentleman was the butler.

Marianne studied him with great interest. Young for a butler, though, she thought. He must have come with glowing recommendations to get such a high post so early in life.

He looked very pleasant, very correct, just like a butler ought to look. She knew everyone in Spiggott Hollow, and without a doubt no male was as good-looking as this gentleman.

"*Too* handsome, in fact," she said, viewing the broad shoulders beneath the dark fustian of his coat. "For a butler."

Bubbling with excitement, Julia had arrived at Darby House earlier that morning to divulge that Lady Randome had hired a young man to replace their old decrepit butler, Boggs. For once, her friend had not been exaggerating. His only flaw, according to Julia, was that he seemed too taciturn and haughty for a mere servant. He wouldn't divulge much about himself.

Marianne righted her straw poke bonnet and straightened her simple sprigged muslin gown adorned with a pink satin ribbon around her bosom. Carrying her empty flower basket and her parasol unfurled against the sharp sunlight, she walked toward the church, where Miss Dew was arranging the flowers on the altar for the Sunday services. She could just as easily have exited from the graveyard through the lych-gate, but her curiosity propelled her past the stranger.

Peeking around the rim of her bonnet, she got a glimpse of shiny chestnut hair and a good-natured, wholly virile face. Even if Marianne didn't think much of the full unfashionable mustache he sported or the wire-rim spectacles, the new man truly was a sight. It was a pity that he was a servant and not an eligible gentleman. *Miss Dew would faint if she saw the bold glance I gave the young man.*

Marianne's heart took a double leap as he looked up, suddenly ceasing his study of the church facade. He saluted her with a curt bow—in Marianne's opinion one not deferential enough for a servant. His smile, however, could not be faulted. It was brighter than the sunlight, and he greeted her cheerfully.

"Good morning. What a lovely day!"

Marianne nodded and swallowed convulsively, speechless in the radiance of his smile. "It is indeed." Never had she met a man with such a merry glint in his eyes. It seemed in direct contrast to his stiff bearing.

Smiling as widely in response—how could one not?— she blushed and hurried into the dark mustiness of the church. It was just as well that she had hastened away, or he might have said something saucy to embarrass her. He had an air about him. She had been fully aware of the unspoken admiration in his eyes. He must not have noticed her uneven gait. Yet. She almost turned around to look at him again through the open door, but she dreaded what she would find in his eyes once he became aware of her imperfection. He glanced over his shoulder and gave her a bold wink. Such a roguish creature, she thought, her blush deepening.

"Where were you all this time?" Miss Dew demanded as they walked home together. Filled with sunshine, the hallway of Darby House looked welcoming. A vase of golden tulips added to the homeliness. Miss Dew carried an armload of flowers, which she promptly began to arrange.

"The weeds were rampant on Mother's grave," Marianne explained while taking off her bonnet.

"You spent nigh an hour in the graveyard," her aunt admonished, and her eyes softened as she viewed her niece.

"I spoke with Mother in a quiet way." Marianne smiled self-consciously, thinking how grateful she was to have her aunt's company. Everything about Annie Dew was round, the shape of her head, the shape of her form. Even the mousy bun at the back of her head was round, as were her pale blue eyes, which lent her a perpetual air of surprise. Of late middle-age, she was Marianne's mother's elder sister who'd remained on the shelf.

Aunt Annie nodded and gave a melancholy smile. "I understand there's such a peace at the graveyard that one is reluctant to leave."

Marianne changed the subject. "Have you met the new butler at Randome's Folly? Julia told me his name is Lester Sherry."

"I saw him outside." Miss Dew's eyes narrowed and her lips worked in outrage. "You didn't stop to converse with him, Marianne?"

Marianne's eyes danced with mischief. "No . . . unless you call a morning greeting a conversation."

"Greeting?" Miss Dew's round face creased in worry. "Is that all?"

"Yes, two words of greeting, and a comment on the weather. You can hardly call that a conversation."

"Well, I suppose that is acceptable. Yet I wouldn't want to get the sharp side of Squire Darby's tongue if he finds out." Miss Dew heaved a visible sigh and continued to arrange the spring flowers in the front parlor. The room was warm and pleasant, the sofas and chairs upholstered in white-and-green-striped satin, and the walls papered with a matching thinner stripe. Interior decor was one of Marianne's interests; even as lofty a peeress as Lady Randome up on the hill often asked her for advice in decorating matters.

"Where's Papa?" Marianne sank down on the sofa and fluffed up a green velvet pillow, her mind still filled with Mr. Sherry's devastating smile.

"Inspecting the new foals." Miss Dew broke off a twig of leaves that spoiled the symmetry of the flower arrangement. "Are you going up to the Folly to view the dead earl?"

Marianne shivered. "I suppose I have to since Lady Randome has been so kind to me in the past."

"She's a tedious featherwit, but that's neither here nor there," Miss Dew said. "She's having a difficult time, and 'tis no more than right that we pay our condolences. The old earl's sisters are there, Mrs. Fitzwilliam and Mrs. Caldway, two ladies I don't know very well. Yet a polite visit must be accomplished."

"The earl was a hard old man. It's difficult to understand why he married a helpless and flustered woman like Lady Randome. She faints at the slightest provocation."

Miss Dew gave Marianne a stern glance. "'Tis not your place to judge them, Marianne. They rubbed along tolerably well. You see, Eudora never argued with the earl, as he could not abide a differing opinion.''

''I'll change my dress before we travel up the hill. It would not do to view a corpse with mud on my knees.'' With a saucy smile at her chaperon's outraged face, Marianne walked upstairs to her bedchamber.

Chapter Two

COSMO AND ECHO LATCH WERE THE ONLY TWINS IN Spiggott Hollow, and slow-witted to boot. They were also the new gardener, Mr. Slocum's, helpers at the Folly. Leith, from his post in the hallway window, sighed in exasperation as he spied the two young men below the terrace that stretched from one end of the house to the other. They were ambling in the direction of the kitchen entrance at the back.

Placing his white-gloved hands behind his back, he studied the twins. They were about twenty years old and wore identical clothes, baggy trousers and gaiters, coarse grimy smocks, and heavy clogs. Floppy hats topped red-haired heads. The bulbous noses, the fleshy lips, and the good-natured—if somewhat vacant—gray eyes were identical. The only way to tell them apart was the fact that Cosmo was cross-eyed on his right eye, while Echo squinted on his left. The two young men were well-meaning and hardworking, and did everything in their power to please Mr. Slocum, who, nevertheless, had torn out many an oily strand of his hair in bouts of exasperation with his underlings.

In confidence Mr. Slocum had informed Leith that he wouldn't have taken the job offer of head gardener had he but met the twins before he accepted the position.

Leith smiled. He quite liked Cosmo and Echo, who were not averse to discussing any rumors that traveled in the village. That's when they could remember the gossip, which wasn't often. Leith hoped to hear something of the letters, but the twins knew nothing of that matter.

A heavy pall hung over the mansion. The body of the earl had arrived to lie in state for two days at the Folly before the funeral. Lady Randome's wails could be heard from her parlor above, and the servants spoke in hushed voices. The doors had been draped with black crepe, and white lilies spread a heavy scent throughout the house.

He heard sounds of voices coming from the passage leading to the kitchen, accompanied by the stomp of heavy clogs. The twins stepped into the hallway, Mrs. Holloway, the housekeeper, fluttering behind them.

"Ah, yes!" Leith said. "You've come to help shifting the body."

"Lor' Randome'll be smellin' like rotten fish by now," Cosmo said, chuckling and twirling his hat between his grimy hands. "Echo says 'e likes th' smell, but—"

Mrs. Holloway wrung her hands and a moan erupted from her before she fled back to the kitchen.

"I believe you ought not discuss the condition of the earl while you're in the house," Leith said censoriously. "In fact, you'd better keep your mouths shut." His back exceedingly stiff, he led the way to the back parlor, where the local midwife was in the process of laying out the earl.

He opened the door and ushered the twins into the room. As if on an unheard cue, they scratched their pink scalps and looked to him for guidance.

"You just do what Mrs. Logan tells you to do," he said, after greeting the midwife.

The twins shuffled over the threshold, and Leith drew a sigh of relief as he closed the door behind them. He had never thought a butler would have so many tasks in one day. Now he had to go down to the cellars and pick out the different wines for dinner. After that he had to supervise the polishing of all the silver for the reception after the funeral. Then he had to make sure the drawing room had enough chairs for the gathering of mourners, and then . . . Yes, never one breath to himself.

After this adventure, he would truly appreciate his own minions' efforts to make him comfortable. Not that he had that many in his lodgings in Half Moon Street, but there was always the loyal Foster, his valet. *I must remember to give him a pay increase when I get back to London, and perhaps a pair of comfortable shoes.*

Leith went to the butler's pantry behind the servants' dining hall and fortified himself with a glass of brandy. The room, with its narrow, austere bed and heavy furniture, never failed to depress him, and he wished the mission were over. Despite his discreet investigation, he'd not been able to discover the offensive love letters.

Perhaps he'd find a way to snoop through Mordecay Follett's personal belongings this afternoon. The burly young man, dark of feature and hair, had left on a drive with Mrs. Fitzwilliam's son, Virgil, a willowy sort of fellow with a lantern jaw. Leith had watched Mordecay as he'd arrived, driving a smart curricle through the village on the previous day. Eager to be in time for the reading of the will, no doubt.

"Why, oh why . . ." Leith whispered, "why did I listen to Grandmama?" He sipped his brandy and looked down at the village, which was shrouded in a sunny haze.

Spiggott Hollow consisted of the church and the vicarage at one end, the mercantile, ten or twelve cottages with vegetable patches, hens, and pigs. Square in the middle of the village was a tavern, the Golden Apple, which served excellent ale. The tavern's name had probably been chosen in honor of the area's many orchards. Even now, in the gilded haze, Leith could see row after neat row of apple and plum trees, gooseberry bushes, and lines of raspberry plants. At the other end of the village presided the green, the pond, and the lazy river. In front of the river stood the tall and narrow Darby House behind its stone wall. The adjoining stables were a beehive of activity.

Leith smiled. Julia Wellesly—as she flitted about fulfilling her aunt's many requests—had mentioned Miss Marianne Darby, her best friend, and Leith was sure he'd gotten a glimpse of the lovely Marianne earlier this morning.

While thinking of Miss Darby, he viewed unseeing a copse of stately elms beyond the vegetable garden at the Folly. She had a dainty-featured face with a pert nose, a dusting of freckles, and wide curious eyes. And if his memory didn't serve him wrong, her eyes had been greenish blue and a ringlet peeking from under her bonnet as gleaming as spun gold. The unspoiled sweetness of her expression had been quite engaging.

Perhaps my sojourn in Spiggott Hollow won't be a complete loss, after all. A bit of dalliance never hurt anyone . . . His gaze moved on. Around the mansion itself, immaculate lawns spread impersonally toward the tree line at the back and down the slope to the village. Formal borders and clipped hedges added to the parklike appearance.

The house proper was made from Kentish ragstone, a rambling structure with additions of every conceivable style and period. Turrets and dormers cluttered the roofline, and what could have been a handsome Palladian estate with soaring columns and arches was ruined by the Gothic facade on the north side. The name "Folly" certainly fit it well.

Leith glanced at the clock on the desk and noticed that an entire hour had passed. Carrying a tray with a bottle and a glass, he sneaked up the stairs to the second floor. Which was Mordecay's bedchamber? One of the footmen had showed him up to his room yesterday. Leith stared at the row of doors in the corridor, reading the name cards in their slots. All the names had not been posted. The large double doors at one end led to the master suite, but there was no clue as to which room was Follett's. One thing was sure, the guests were all staying on the same floor. Mrs. Holloway had ordered all the spare bedrooms to be aired.

He heard female voices coming from the wide curving marble stairs—maids, if he didn't mistake their broad accents. He tried the first door handle and prayed no one would be inside. The room was dim, due to the drawn curtains.

Until his eyes adjusted, he could not see if anyone was within. He closed the door gently just before the maids passed in the corridor. The room was quiet, and Leith decided he could just as well see if this was the chamber he wanted. He stepped toward the tallboy in one corner.

"Can I be of assistance?" a clear female voice inquired.

Leith stiffened in surprise and turned slowly toward the sweet voice. On the edge of the bed sat a young woman, partly shielded by the bed hangings. He noticed another form on the bed, the legs covered with a blanket. At the last moment he remembered that he was a servant. He bowed in humiliation.

"I'm terribly sorry. I must be in the wrong room. Mr. Follett asked for refreshment." He edged toward the door.

The young woman rose and walked to the windows where she pulled the curtains aside. A moan came from the bed.

"Marianne, the sunlight hurts my eyes," a querulous voice said from the depths of the pillows.

Leith saw that the prostrate form was an older woman dressed in black mourning weeds. Evidently the young lady was Marianne Darby. Her hair shone guinea gold, and her heart-shaped face was far sweeter than he recalled. As he gazed into her wide eyes something struck his heart, a sudden blinding pain that dissolved into a warm softness.

"Mrs. Fitzwilliam, the butler is about to leave." She gave Leith a frank stare. "I daresay you gave us quite a turn with your quiet entry, Sherry."

"I . . . thought Mr. Follett might be asleep, but he distinctly asked me—"

"That's neither here nor there. We don't require a bottle of claret, and this is not Mr. Follett's room."

The older woman braced herself on her elbow. Her eyes were red from much crying, her dark hair untidy. Silver strands wove from forehead to nape, and Leith noticed the beaky, protruding nose. "Claret? I could use a nip of that since you're here, Sherry."

She peered nearsightedly at Leith, who wished himself

to be elsewhere. He remembered to bow obsequiously and set the tray down by the bed. Turning the corkscrew expertly, he soon had uncorked the bottle.

"How are the funeral preparations going?" Mrs. Fitzwilliam touched a handkerchief to her nose, but Leith only had eyes for Marianne. The light from the windows made an aura around her slight form, and her eyes were a luminous blue green, the color of the sunlight playing in seawater. He couldn't find his voice while looking into those calm, clear pools.

Only after tearing his gaze away could he reply. "All is satisfactory, Mrs. Fitzwilliam." He moved toward the door, but hesitated, knowing he ought to wait until dismissed.

The older woman huffed and worked herself into a sitting position. She sipped the wine gingerly. "This was timely." She sighed and pressed the handkerchief to her eyes. "You can leave now, Sherry. No need to gawk."

Leith gave Marianne an apologetic shrug and headed toward the door. She followed him, saying, "Is there a problem?"

Beautiful and shrewd, too, Leith thought as he put his hand on the doorknob and stepped out. The corridor was a reprieve. "No, I mistook the room, that's all. Excuse me, but I must fetch another bottle now."

She narrowed her eyes speculatively, and he realized she didn't quite believe him. A butler would surely know the location of the houseguests. . . .

He wished he could engage her in a conversation. He would before long, he vowed.

"Is that man still here?" The question came fretfully from the bed.

"He's about to leave." Marianne waited patiently in the door opening until he'd reached the top of the stairs.

Leith thought he'd grown two left feet, and he flushed, something he'd *never* done before. Could she see through his disguise? Thank God he'd made sure the false mustache was secure before he went upstairs.

Just as he reached the landing a lady's scream echoed in the hallway below. Leith bounded down the curving oaken steps. Between the globe-shaped spindles in the balustrade, he saw the form of a female on the settle by the front door. One glance told him she was Lady Randome. A servant was fluttering a handkerchief over her face, and another arrived with a bottle of hartshorn in one hand.

Marianne was close behind him. "What happened?" she asked, and hastened to help the servants reviving her ladyship. As his humble station demanded, Leith remained in the background.

"She went into the parlor to make sure all was . . . well, right with the earl, Miss Darby," said Bert, the footman. "She came screaming out of there."

Leith recalled Cosmo and Echo and wondered if their presence had frightened Lady Randome. Where were the blasted twins? He opened the parlor door discreetly, but no one was inside. Two branches of candles glowed eerily at the head of the casket. Everything seemed to be in order. He glanced out the window and saw the twins digging a border at the opposite end of the garden. Relieved, he returned to the foyer, where the countess showed signs of calming down—thanks to Miss Darby's capable ministrations. Again that flush of warmth flooded his heart, and he felt an urge to examine his tumultuous feelings in private. But he couldn't withdraw at this point.

The widow leaned limply against the maid's comforting arm. She was dressed from head to toe in black. Her gray hair was scraped back into an unbecoming bun, and her face was as pale as a fish belly. Yet Leith noticed that the face still held some modicum of beauty—a fine bone structure and a regally tilted nose.

"Where am I?" Lady Randome croaked, gripping the hartshorn bottle between bony fingers.

"In the hallway, milady. Something frightened you. Can you recall what?" Marianne asked kindly. She ordered the footman to fetch a blanket, then cradled Lady Randome's head on her lap to make the old lady more comfortable.

Not only is she beautiful, but she has the disposition of a saint, Leith thought, unable to tear his eyes from Miss Darby's lovely face.

Lady Randome heaved herself to a sitting position and leaned against the unyielding back of the settle. "It's a private matter, between me, and Randome . . . and Mrs. Caldway."

The earl's younger sister, the romantic fool, Leith thought.

"Yoo-hoo, are you talking about me?" Kitty Caldway cried out as she glided out of the back parlor, hands clasped together as if in prayer and wisps of fabric trailing from every curve of her plump body.

"Oh, go away, Kitty! You've caused too much trouble as it is," Lady Randome said.

Mrs. Caldway didn't take the hint, but continued all the way to the settle.

Lady Randome pressed her handkerchief to her eyes. "I'm going upstairs for a rest, and I don't want to be disturbed." She noticed Leith and beckoned him to her side.

"Sherry, lead me upstairs if you please. I've had quite

enough upheaval for one day.'' She gripped his arm and started shuffling across the floor.

"What is the matter?'' Marianne probed. "I've never seen Lady Randome that shocked.''

Mrs. Caldway's voice rose toward the high ceiling as Leith conducted his employer upstairs. "Why, I believed Eudora would enjoy reading her old love letters to the earl. It seems that he treasured them for over thirty years.''

"Love letters?'' Marianne echoed.

"Yes . . . only they turned out to be written by someone else—by some young infatuated girl, oh, so long ago. I found the bundle in the old copper urn in the library, of all places. Who would have thought Egbert would have kept them there, and why? They were quite . . . er, torrid.'' She gave an audible sigh. "How romantic, don't you think? I recited one to Eudora, and she got most upset.''

The letters! Leith staggered under the ever-heavier burden of Lady Randome as the words floated up to him. As they reached the landing she sagged against him with a moan, and he had to lift her into his arms.

"Where are the letters now?'' Marianne demanded.

"Oh, my. I was going to show Eudora that I'd placed them in Egbert's hands, but they were gone.''

Dammit! Leith almost dropped his burden. He wanted to drop it and speed downstairs in search of the letters, but it was unthinkable.

As soon as he'd settled Lady Randome against the pillows of her bed and left her in the tender care of her maid, he hurried downstairs. The foyer was empty, and he went stealthily to the parlor door.

The candles gave an eerie light, and Leith started

guiltily as he noticed Miss Darby's slender form by the coffin. She lifted her gaze to his as he came inside.

"No, they are not here, if that's what you were looking for, Sherry."

Leith cleared his throat. Again he found himself in a spot where he ought not to be. "I wanted to make sure everything was in order here," he said lamely.

"It is," Miss Darby said, and followed him outside. "I have no idea what those letters meant to Lord Randome. They have disappeared." She smiled at him, a smile that rendered him speechless. "Sherry, please fetch my shawl. I'm going home."

He did as she had bid, then stared, from behind a curtain, at her as she walked down the hill. The slight irregularity of her stride lent a certain grace to her movements, a grace that was all her own.

He returned to the butler's pantry and sat down heavily in the only armchair in the room. As his squalling emotions settled, one fact shone brightly in his mind. He'd fallen in love. He'd fallen like a stone in the sea of her calm blue-green eyes, and he was still sinking. For once he understood what the poets had described as love—struck by Cupid's arrow. He knew without a doubt that he'd found the lady with whom he wanted to spend the rest of his days.

Chapter Three

TWO HOURS LATER, WHEN HE'D DESCENDED MOMENtarily from the euphoria of love, Leith realized he'd failed to search Mordecay Follett's room. Frowning, he rubbed his chin. He hadn't even set eyes on the young wastrel this evening, only Lord Randome's teary-eyed sisters and wife, besides the lovely Marianne. The day hadn't been totally wasted, after all, he thought with a chuckle. He knew exactly what to do this evening . . . he would write a letter.

The next morning Marianne opened an envelope and pulled out one sheet of paper. Puzzled, she read:

> *Oh, fair beauty, you dazzle my eye!*
> *The world stopped, and why . . . ?*
> *I met you.*
> *My heart palpitated with gladness.*
> *Sweet Marianne, don't be shy*
> *Let us experience this madness.*
> *'Tis Love!*

Marianne dropped the note, exclaiming, "What drivel!"

Miss Dew entered at that moment. "Drivel?"

Marianne pointed at the note. "Swinton Langley, no doubt. He doesn't have an ounce of poetry in him. It's the most dreadful poem I've ever read."

Miss Dew didn't hesitate to pick it up. She chuckled. "I admit it's in poor taste, but at least it shows you have an admirer."

Marianne glared. "He didn't have the decency to sign it."

"A silent admirer," Miss Dew corrected herself. "How intriguing." She gave her charge a wide smile. "You'll be wed yet, Marianne, my girl. You just wait and see."

"You possess an overly romantic heart." Followed by Miss Dew, Marianne sat down in the parlor with her embroidery frame. "I have no intention of marrying Swinton Langley. As soon as I see him, I'll advise him not to send me any more missives, signed or otherwise."

Miss Dew sighed. "I think it's sweet. Evidently he's too shy to approach you directly."

Marianne gave her chaperon another glower. "He's anything but shy, Aunt Annie, and well you know it. A more pompous bore I have yet to meet."

"I'll allow he's a trifle long-winded at times." Miss Dew eyed her charge critically. "But I cannot blame the gentleman for being taken in by your fair beauty."

"Fiddlesticks! No gentleman in London would look at me twice." She viewed the needlepoint in her lap. She was making new covers for the dining-room chairs, a wreath of flowers on a pale green background.

Miss Dew chose her words carefully, knowing that Marianne still hurt inside at the rejection she had suffered in London. "There are so many young misses in London, my dear. Only the very fairest will stand out."

"My infirmity—"

"Rubbish! You must stop thinking about your hip injury. No man worth his salt will pay attention to it. Swinton Langley might be a bore, but he has never as much as indicated that he finds you less than perfect."

Marianne's eyes brightened. "You're the kindest of souls, Aunt Annie, but it doesn't detract from the fact that I abhor Swinton Langley. We would never suit."

"Perhaps one of the watering places would present an opportunity—"

"Desist, do! I don't care if I ever marry. I'm perfectly happy looking after Father."

Miss Dew's lips pursed with disapproval as she gave her niece a sideways glance. "You cannot fool yourself forever. What you need is a family of your own."

"I know Father doesn't like Swinton Langley, but he admits he's so very *proper,* a character trait of which Father approves greatly. He has hinted that he wouldn't be averse to a match between us."

The squire entered at that moment. He was large and heavyset, with a florid face and hair as bristly as the fur of a wild boar. "Did I hear you mention that mincing fellow Langley?" As Marianne nodded the squire sat down and spread out his newspaper on the table. "He tries to ingratiate himself with me by pretending to be interested in horses. A worse seat I've yet to see! Sits a horse like a veritable hay sack. Besides, horses make him wheeze."

"Surely you cannot blame him for having a weak chest, Algie," Miss Dew admonished. "Mr. Langley is a harmless young man."

Algernon Darby gave his daughter a glance from over

the rim of the spectacles he used when reading. His eyes were the same sea-green color as Marianne's. "He has asked to be allowed to court you properly. What are you going to do?"

Marianne's eyes widened. "You leave the decision to me?"

The squire shrugged. "You know my opinion on the matter; he would make a suitable husband, but 'tis your life and your decision, m'dear."

Marianne smiled. "Thank you, Papa. But I think you know my answer—"

The door opened and Willow, the butler, stepped inside, his features set in his usual mournful mask. "Mr. Swinton Langley."

Marianne wished she had told Willow she wasn't at home to morning callers. She sighed as she observed the slender young man entering the room. His narrow face had a perpetually shifty expression and his complexion was pasty, as if he spent all his time indoors. Which he did. His eyes were brown and bearing an expression of disapproval. Swinton Langley walked with both feet on the earth and preferably on paths untouched by common people. His precise attire, including an excessively stiff neckcloth, told its own story of "starch." Langley was the only eligible man in Spiggott Hollow, and he knew it. He lived with his old mother in a decrepit mansion along the road to Tunbridge Wells, but the way he tilted his nose one would think he lived a life of bottomless wealth. Truth was that Mrs. Langley and son scraped by on a small inheritance after Swinton's father had died five years before. Marianne's dowry was a remedy that could miraculously cure Swinton's every woe.

"Good morning," he greeted nasally, and directed an infatuated smile in Marianne's direction. He bowed to

Miss Dew and nodded to the squire, who snorted in return. "I pray I find you in the best of health," Langley went on, speaking to no one in particular as he was standing in the middle of the room. He swiveled his head with difficulty toward Marianne as the high shirt points dug into his cheeks.

"Sit down, young man," Miss Dew said kindly. "How's your mother?"

"She's lying down with a sick headache this morning." He raised one bony finger. "That reminds me, when we went to Tunbridge Wells last week, Mother had the most terrible migraine. She went into the cloth merchant's shop and—"

"That's all very well, m'boy," said the squire irritably. "Want to inspect my new hunter?"

"—and the pain made her so blind she walked straight into a stack of cloth bolts, which overturned in the most distressing manner. I've never been more mortified." He took a deep breath. "I actually had to get down on my hands and knees and assist Mother in her swoon. She's so very helpless at times. Then—"

"If you excuse me," the squire muttered, and fled from the room.

"—then I had to carry her outside, where she—instead of reviving—went into a deeper swoon, which required her doctor's firm attention. Why, I've been bound to her bedside ever since, holding her hand."

"Very kind and proper of you, Mr. Langley," Miss Dew said, and bit off a piece of embroidery yarn.

"Mother—"

"Are you going to attend Lord Randome's funeral, Swinton?" Marianne hastened to interrupt.

"Certainly. One has to do the proper thing, don't you agree?" He crossed his legs delicately and stared into space. "I heard some shocking gossip. It appears that the earl had received a handful of very improper letters—"

"Really, Swinton. One shouldn't listen to gossip, especially if it isn't true."

Langley continued unperturbed. "But it is. Mother was so distressed she immediately traveled up to the Folly to express her sympathies to Lady Randome." A sigh trembled on his lips. "One hears that the earl had some very *fast* goings-on in his youth. Some young lady *swooned* over him. Mother says—"

"Mere hearsay. No one except Mrs. Caldway had seen the letters, and you know how scatterbrained she is," Marianne said.

He changed the subject. "I hear Lady Randome has hired a new butler."

"I have met him." Marianne remembered a pair of smiling deep blue eyes and thought uncharitably that Mr. Sherry had more charm in his little finger than Swinton had in his entire body. "It isn't wise to listen to gossip," she reminded him.

He started at her words, and two red spots glowed on his cheeks. "Gossip about the butler? Who's mentioning gossip?"

"Well, I know for a fact that he's both young and personable," Miss Dew said.

"Hmmph!" said Mr. Langley. "I hear he's been flirting with all the barmaids at the Golden Apple, and I, for one, cannot hold with such improper conduct!"

Miss Dew laughed. "Don't take on so. I'm sure an hour of innocent flirting won't ruin the barmaids. They positively *thrive* on such behavior."

Swinton Langley's face crumpled as if she'd slapped him. His back stiffened as if he thought flirting an utterly repulsive act.

Marianne picked up the poem she had received earlier and handed it to Swinton. "Did you write this?"

He glanced at it, his eyes bulging as he read. "Miss Darby! How could you think that I would be so ill-mannered as to send you love notes without having your father's permission to court you?"

His nose quivered with outrage, and Marianne could barely suppress a chuckle. "Then who wrote it?"

"I must say I'm terribly shocked!" He turned to Miss Dew. "You must guard Miss Darby better. We cannot have uncouth young men pressing their filthy attentions on her."

Miss Dew laughed. "I thought the poem was rather sweet." She winked imperceptibly to Marianne, who frowned in vexation.

"I'm well capable of looking after myself," Marianne said in no uncertain tones. Who had written the love poem if Swinton hadn't? She should have known better than to suspect him. He would never do anything that improper, or would he?

"Mother always says a young lady should be locked in her room until she is ready to enter the church on her wedding day." He looked into space. "I tend to agree with her. Mother always had such fine judgment."

"Isn't she lonely without your attendance this morning?" Marianne asked with a shrewd glance at her suitor.

"She's too ill, alas. The trip to the Folly wore her out. It distressed me so much that I had palpitations when I saw her so pale against the pillows. I had to go out for a few minutes—to visit you, Miss Darby, and gather strength from our friendly companionship. You have been much on my mind." He moved a space closer to her on the sofa.

Marianne shuddered, and inched farther away.

"But I must not neglect Mother much longer. I'd better be there to keep an eye on things. Our housekeeper—yes, there's the most shocking tidbit about Mrs. Erskine—"

"You can tell us next time," Miss Dew said briskly. She went to give the bellrope a tug. "We must not detain you when Mrs. Langley is so very indisposed."

Willow entered, closely followed by Julia Wellesly. He didn't have time to announce her presence before she bounded into the room. "There you are! Marianne, had you forgotten that you're supposed to accompany me to the vicarage to discuss the church bazaar? We must decide on the final arrangement, and you know I can't go without you." She plopped down on the sofa beside Marianne without as much as a look at Swinton Langley, who was leaving with the butler. Langley and Julia Wellesly could not abide each other.

"You're wearing a new gown, Marianne. How lovely." She closely inspected the light blue muslin gown with tiny white dots and a white sash. Her eyes twinkled as she whispered, "Are you wearing it to impress Swinton Langley?"

Marianne jabbed her best friend with an elbow. "If you're here to tease me, I won't help you with the bazaar."

Julia made a moue that blossomed into a smile. "If it weren't for you, this bazaar would never come about. The vicar is shockingly disorganized. His idea of fixing the problem with the leaking church roof would be to place buckets under the leaks."

Marianne chuckled ruefully. "Don't flatter me to get your way! You could always ask Sherry for help." Marianne gave her friend a sly look.

"Oh, yes . . . he's very nice, but there's something

strange about him." Julia set her face into thoughtful lines. "I find him in the most unexpected places, like in the pantry, which is Cook's domain, or in the linen closet rooting in a box, an area which belongs solely to Mrs. Holloway. He might make powerful enemies there. And his hands are so *white* and well manicured, as if he'd never done any hard work before, like polishing the silver."

"When did you look closely at Sherry's hands?" Marianne asked pointedly. She pretended not to care, but her curiosity knew no bounds.

"When Lady Randome interviewed him for the position. I happened to be in the parlor at that time, and they were speaking in the library. Lady Randome has such a carrying voice that I heard the entire conversation, and she complimented him on his clean hands. I took a look later. Furthermore Lady Randome commented on Sherry's unfashionable mustache, and he said he'd grown it to cover a scar. He said he would not consider shaving it off."

"Hmm, it's a bit odd. He is a very unbutlerish butler."

"It seemed this morning that the downstairs maid, Lottie, had to *teach* him how to polish the silver." She laughed wickedly. "Their heads were awfully close together, you know."

"Shame on you, Julia, you've been spying."

"No such thing! I was sewing, and then I had to look for my missing pair of scissors—"

"In the servants' hall? I presume that's where they were working on the silver."

Julia blushed prettily. "You must admit he's devilishly handsome," she whispered out of earshot of Miss Dew.

Marianne smiled conspiratorially. "I can't deny that.

A veritable heart-crusher.'' She rose calmly and put away her sewing. It was difficult to believe that the buxom Julia Wellesly was the spying kind. She meant nothing by it, but she was shockingly curious. Perhaps it was due to her longing for Gregory, and the escape from the Folly she would make on his arm.

Marianne thought Julia was lovely, but Julia complained that she looked like an elephant with her impressive height and sturdy frame. Her round face was cheerful, and her golden-brown eyes mercurial. Due to her dubious status in the Randome household, she wore modest clothes in dull colors that didn't enhance her pale skin and pale brown hair.

"Where are you off to?" asked Miss Dew as she returned to the room after speaking with Willow in the hallway.

"You must come, Miss Dew. Marianne has promised to help me with the last details of the bazaar.''

Miss Dew nodded, and the three ladies were soon walking through the village, parasols spread against the sunlight. The proprietor of the Golden Apple was sweeping the steps outside his door. He doffed his hat and smiled as they passed.

At the other end of the village, by the church, they encountered Mrs. Caldway, Lord Randome's youngest sister, and Mordecay Follett. The tiny bereaved lady was leaning heavily on the young man's arm as they walked slowly toward the carriage waiting outside the church.

"Good morning," Miss Dew directed at Mrs. Caldway's veiled face. "I'm surprised to see you outdoors, Mrs. Caldway, considering—''

"I worried so about my brother. I had to make sure the church would be ready for the funeral tomorrow." She fumbled with a handkerchief under the veil. According to

Miss Dew, Mrs. Caldway had always been a sentimental woman, "a veritable watering pot." "The family vault is so dreadfully cold and dark. He'll be miserable there," the lady continued.

Miss Dew had the situation firmly under control as she spoke briskly, "You must recall that the earl was fond of the outdoors when he was at the Folly. A bit of cold never stopped him from hunting."

"How right you are," Mrs. Caldway said in a broken voice.

She looked frail in her mourning draperies, and Mordecay looked positively sinister in his black suit of clothes, Marianne thought. He possessed a handsome enough physique, but there was something about his dark eyes and heavy eyebrows that gave Marianne an uneasy feeling in the pit of her stomach. He wore his dark hair combed forward in the Brutus style and plastered to his head with pomade. Only one curl spiraled affectedly over his forehead. He bowed to the ladies, but the hardness around his mouth never softened.

"Mordecay has been a rock in my sea of despair," Mrs. Caldway continued, clasping Follett's sturdy arm harder. "I was delighted when he decided to stay here for a few days after the funeral, to support us all. His kindness is saintly, since Randome didn't bequeath a penny to the poor boy."

Follett bared his teeth in a parody of a smile, and Julia clutched Marianne's arm in disgust. "Let's continue our mission," she whispered. "The vicar is waiting."

"How are you, Miss Darby?" Mordecay asked with another baring of teeth.

"Very well, thank you," Marianne said briskly, realizing that Swinton Langley was not devious, like this young man. She gave her chaperon a speaking glance.

"We must tend to our errand," Miss Dew said. "Such a nice day to be abroad, don't you think? Such a happy day."

With a sob, Mrs. Caldway staggered forward, and Miss Dew saw her faux pas too late. Her lips worked, but no apology came out. Follet helped Mrs. Caldway into the barouche, and Miss Dew said a hasty good-bye.

"She'll never forgive me," Miss Dew muttered as she led the way across the churchyard toward the vicarage. "Never speak to me again."

"Don't take on so," Marianne admonished. "You're perfectly right, you know. About the morning. It is a lovely day."

As they reached the front porch of the vicarage, they heard male voices inside. Marianne was the first to discover Lester Sherry, the Randome butler.

"Good morning," greeted the Reverend Otterby as he saw them. He gave a beaming smile. "Come in and meet Mr. Sherry. He's promised to help mend and erect the trestle tables for the bazaar."

"We've met before," Marianne said, viewing the tall man in front of her. "Isn't Mr. Sherry supposed to be at his post at the Folly?"

"It's my half day off. When Miss Wellesly explained about the bazaar, I realized I could help." His smile spread like a warm mantle around her. "I hope you don't mind."

"Oh, no," Marianne said, blushing. The man had an uncanny knack for making her feel self-conscious. "Why didn't you tell me?" she whispered to Julia, who only shrugged and shook her head.

He was carrying a wooden toolbox in one hand and gestured toward the door. "Do you care to show me where the tables are kept?"

He smiled again, and Marianne's heart beat faster. He truly had the most engaging grin she'd ever seen. A most endearing man. There was almost something familiar about him . . . as if she'd seen him before. The vicar was gesticulating vigorously, thereby catching Miss Dew's attention. As they discussed the various details of the bazaar, Marianne found herself walking alongside the butler.

"It's quite a glorious morning," Sherry said noncommittally. "I think Kent is a very beautiful corner of this isle."

"You're not from these parts, then?" Marianne asked. She didn't really want to get involved in a conversation with the man since he rattled her composure, but to keep silent seemed rude.

"No . . . yes, well, I've worked in London, and in Yorkshire—a much more rugged terrain."

"We don't encounter many strangers in Spiggott Hollow. After what I hear, you've created quite a stir in the village."

"Hmm," he said with a wicked smile. "Gossip travels fast, faster than I can create it."

"I should say it's disgraceful to be the center of village gossip."

"Since I am a stranger, anything that I do will create gossip."

Marianne gave a reluctant smile, even though she resented admitting that his charm was working on her. "It is kind of you to help us with the bazaar."

"I'm a fortunate fellow to be here." His eyes held a wealth of suggestions, and Marianne inhaled sharply.

They arrived at the large wooden shed partly concealed by a lilac hedge. Stack upon stack of tables took up most of the space. The sexton arrived and helped Sherry to pull them out.

Meanwhile, Marianne watched the butler's strong body at work. She viewed his hands suspiciously, remembering Julia's observation that he had uncommonly clean hands. Julia was right. Marianne could have sworn the nails had had a manicure not too long ago. And his hair. It wasn't cut in an uneven shag like the hairdos of the villagers. The proprietor of the Golden Apple was also the barber of Spiggott Hollow, and Marianne suspected he poured a glass of ale much smoother than he cut a fringe of hair.

Ten minutes later Sherry bent down to inspect the tabletops and trestles, and beckoned Marianne to his side.

She bent down beside him.

"I believe the wood is rotten," Sherry said. "There isn't much I can do except build new trestles." He got down on his haunches and gently pulled off one of the trestle legs. He smelled of sunshine and summer, and a warm virile scent mixed with perspiration that came from honest hard work. Marianne had never before been so close to a man to smell his unique scent.

He pointed at the break. "Does the vicar have lumber that I could use?"

"I . . . I don't know," she said dreamily. "You must ask him."

Her gaze met his and locked, and Marianne felt as if she were sinking into him, reading his every thought and every nuance of his emotions. She read admiration, confusion, excitement—all the things she was experiencing herself at that moment.

"How clever he is," Julia said, and she sounded so far

away. In a daze, Marianne could not take her eyes off his smiling face.

"We might as well make some new trestles," said the vicar. "The available funds should cover the cost of some lumber."

Much too rapidly the butler rose, while Marianne wished she could stay by his side for the remainder of the day. The air was gently perfumed with the scent of flowers, and the sunlight played in the foliage above. "Such peace," she whispered.

He nodded, and his eyes grew serious and probing. Marianne blushed, and forced herself upright. It wouldn't do to exchange intimate glances with a butler! What had gotten into her?

She turned away abruptly, and the vicar started a conversation with Mr. Sherry.

"Come, Julia. There's nothing else for us to do here. Let's see how the flowers are faring on Mother's grave," she said breathlessly, and hurried down the path to the graveyard.

"What's the hurry?" Julia complained as she tried to keep up with her friend. "Isn't he divine? Would that he were a gentleman!"

Marianne agreed wholeheartedly, but said nothing. From the corner of her eye, she noticed that Sherry was following their progress with his gaze.

"They look wilted," Miss Dew commented as she arrived sometime later. "You must water these flowers or they'll never last."

"I'll fetch the watering can," Marianne said, wanting to be alone with her thoughts.

But when she arrived at the pump, the can was gone. She would have to fetch one in the toolshed right behind the mortuary. Reliving the moments she had spent with

Sherry, she was filled with agitation. It would not do to fall in love with a common butler! As she arrived at the shed she could hear someone humming a tune inside. Then there was a crash, and a curse singed the air.

She looked inside to see if someone needed her assistance. The only man there was Sherry, and another curse erupted from his lips as he stared at his bloodied thumb. He stared at her, and she stared at him as the revelation dawned. He didn't know how to use a hammer. Before she could make clear her observation to him, he'd taken two steps toward her, his arms held wide. With a question in his eyes, he swept her into his embrace. She swayed with shock as he pressed a very hot and demanding kiss to her lips.

Chapter Four

THE WORLD TILTED BEFORE MARIANNE'S EYES, WOVEN baskets hanging from the ceiling twirling crazily above her head, and wooden beams spinning. Dizzy and confused, she closed her eyes, and she would have fallen if Sherry hadn't kept his strong arms around her. His lips caressed hers, soft and warm, gentle, yet curiously demanding. His bushy mustache tickled her chin. He was pulling her senses inside out with his touch, and Marianne had never experienced a more exquisite feeling. For a moment she let herself be swept away on the tide of sensation, losing all thought. Then sanity returned and she tore herself with difficulty from his powerful embrace. In the last moment she stopped herself from slapping his face.

"How dare you!" She wished her admonition had come out with more authority than the pitiful croak that passed her lips. Her senses still reeled from the shock of his kiss, and she swallowed hard to gain control of herself. She wiped her mouth and repeated her words, now with more strength. "How *dare* you."

At first he gave her a warm, triumphant smile, then his face fell into lines of distress. He dropped his hands to his side. "I'm terribly sorry," he said in a rush, as if he'd just remembered something. Perhaps he'd recalled that he was a butler. Butlers did not kiss ladies above their station. . . .

This one evidently did, Marianne thought, much shaken. She wished she could gather her thoughts for a harsher rebuke, but all she was aware of was her weak and trembling legs.

"You've taken shocking liberties with me, Mr. Sherry." Her voice began to shake with anger. "If I tell Lady Randome about this, you'll be out of her employ."

"I implore you, Miss Darby, to forgive me. I completely lost my head." He gestured gracefully toward her face. "I could not resist the temptation of your sweet lips—if I may be so bold as to say so, and I don't know what recklessness overcame me."

He truly looked contrite, and Marianne—who could never hold a grudge—nodded slowly. "Very well. Don't mention it. If you ever do this again, I will certainly speak up."

He looked so sad, but a sparkle lit his eyes momentarily, then was gone. Not wholly contrite, she thought, but he had begged her forgiveness most sincerely. Another lady might have run out of the shed, screaming, but she wasn't the hysterical kind, nor would she faint at the smallest upheaval.

"I don't know if I should believe you, Mr. Sherry. It seems to me that you are a different character than you appear to be. Why, you don't know how to use a hammer, and if I recall correctly, you do not seem to understand your butler duties very well. Julia Wellesly said—"

He raised his hands in mock horror. "Have mercy, Miss Darby. My grandmother said I'm the most impractical person in the Sherry family, but if Lady Randome finds out, my employment might be in jeopardy." He lowered his tone a notch. "I scrape along tolerably well, Miss Darby. You see, I'm rather apt at covering up my faux pas."

"Like right now, you mean?" Marianne said with a pinch of sarcasm.

"Miss Darby!" he exclaimed. "Haven't I suffered enough? Don't make me squirm with guilt." He took a step closer, and Marianne felt his powerful pull on her senses. "Please forgive me again, but I can't express my admiration enough. You're the loveliest lady I've ever set eyes on."

Marianne could not help but laugh. "Mr. Sherry, you're a rogue, a man wholly without principle. I don't believe a word of your flattery. You'd better be silent from now on, or I might change my mind about reporting you."

"You wound me deeply, Miss Darby. Every word I said was true." Leith sucked on the wound and studied the beautiful face before him for signs of softening, but he saw only bewilderment. A blush suffused her translucent skin, and her plump lower lip trembled as if she were about to cry. But no tears glittered in her blue-green eyes, only anger tinged with wry humor. His heart thundered wildly, his every nerve ending yearning to touch her again. How could such a slip of a woman incite such strong feelings in his heart? It was puzzling, to say the least.

She glanced at his injured thumb. "You're hurt. Let me wrap a clean handkerchief around the wound." She delved into her reticule that dangled from a twisted cord around her wrist. She didn't meet his gaze as she wrapped his thumb, knotting the ends together carefully. "I suppose you kiss ladies at every opportunity," she said, breaking into his thoughts. He longed to sweep her off her feet and into his arms, where he would kiss her into oblivion. Unprincipled desire, he admonished himself. Dishonorable behavior—not the way to treat a lady. What had gotten into him? He'd better be careful. He had never humiliated a lady before, and he certainly wouldn't start now. It was as if his new identity made him more reckless. Yes—he had to remember his role. If he lost his employment, his mission to find the love letters would be at risk.

"I only kiss ladies when they are as attractive as you are, Miss Darby." He meant it, but that didn't pardon his ill-mannered behavior.

She gasped, her blush deepening. "You're impossible, Mr. Sherry. I shall not speak with you further." She glanced around helplessly, and he wondered what she was looking for. Emboldened by her obvious confusion, he continued, "A beauty like you must be quite used to such homage as I just paid you."

Her eyebrows rose. "Homage?" she scoffed. "Attack, more likely." She shook her head. "No, Mr. Sherry, *gentlemen* don't take advantage of ladies. They do not kiss without permission, nor do they court a lady without the consent of her father."

She moved toward the door, purposefully glancing along the hooks on the wall. "Have you seen the watering can?"

"Outside, behind the door." He moved ahead of her and retrieved the metal can, but when she tried to take it from him, he held it out of reach. "Let me carry it for you."

She made a moue, then shrugged. "If you must impose your presence on me further."

With a bow, he fell behind her on the path. "I'd like to recover what dignity I have lost in your eyes, Miss Darby."

He shamelessly viewed her slender frame, noting her straight back and her nicely rounded hips under the simple muslin gown. A ringlet curling away from the prim bun at the nape gave her a vulnerable air. Her long slim throat enhanced the impression of vulnerability. . . . She walked gracefully, with that slight jig in her gait that endeared her to him. She seemed reluctant to walk ahead of him, and he wondered why.

Marianne felt his eyes on her. What an insolent man! She blushed at the thought that he was right behind her, taking in every nuance of her uneven gait. No wonder he'd tried to take liberties with her. He figured that she—with her disability—would be grateful for any attention shown to her. If only she hadn't responded so shockingly to his touch . . . if only he were a gentleman. If only someone more suitable, someone other than an impudent butler with eyes as blue as the sky, found her attractive enough to kiss her, she would ask for nothing else.

They walked under the trees toward the graves.

"Miss Darby, have you ever wondered what it would feel like to be struck by lightning?"

He was speaking to her again, forgetting his place as easily as if she were the dairymaid at Randome's Folly. She didn't hold his lower station in contempt; it was just that he acted so completely without the usual reticence of servants. It was as if he were used to conversing with the gentry. "Lightning? What an odd thing to ask, I'm sure. No, I've never wondered."

"I know it's unforgivable that I kissed you, Miss Darby, but I was struck by lightning. That's what truly happened."

"For a proper butler, you're very glib, Mr. Sherry. Our butler at Darby House barely ever says a word unless he's about to announce someone, or speak up about the weather."

"A dull fellow, by all accounts. Didn't you feel that bolt of fire, Miss Darby?" he continued. "A special feeling like that doesn't come often in life, perhaps only once."

"What difference does it make?" she said, her anger kindling anew. "If I were you, Mr. Sherry, I would be very careful what I say in front of Miss Dew. If she finds out what you just said and did to me, she would *run* up the hill to Lady Randome. You would be out of Randome's Folly within the hour, with no reference."

"That might be a relief," he muttered under his breath.

She stopped abruptly in front of him on the path and demanded his attention. "*What* did you just say, Mr. Sherry?"

"That would be intolerable," he said, and smiled that sunny smile, inspiring her to blush once again.

"You're a scoundrel, and no mistake," she said, and hurried to join her aunt and Julia Wellesly, who had weeded the flower border.

"That took an eternity," said Miss Dew, eyeing the Randome butler with suspicion as he poured water from a heavy pail on the path into the watering can.

"I couldn't find the can, but Mr. Sherry helped me." Marianne lowered her gaze lest her aunt read the guilt in her eyes.

The butler bowed deferentially. "I must go back to mending those tables."

Marianne's gaze followed him as he hurried up the path toward the shed. Shaken to the marrow, she could barely gather her thoughts. Her encounter with the Randome butler had turned her world upside down, and she wasn't sure it could be righted again. His kiss had awakened feelings that she hadn't known existed in her heart. Vague yearnings, yes, but not this volcano spewing forth sensations as hot as lava, and just as devastating. His analogy to the lightning might have been simple, but so true. Had he really felt such an attraction? Well, if he had, why had he burdened her with a confession? They could never have a future together.

Leith watched the ladies from the door opening of the shed. Insects buzzed around him, but he was only aware of Marianne Darby's pale blue dress and bent head as she watered the plants. Lighted by the sun from behind, she looked as if she'd been struck by lightning, the light lingering in a warm halo around her. Oh, she was lovely, an unspoiled wildflower that didn't draw much attention to itself, unless one took the time to look closer. No wonder he'd been carried away by his feelings. He'd handled the situation badly, but he'd been so eager to discover some response in her eyes. Dismay he'd seen, and some humor, yes, but love? No. Fool, he chided himself. *How could you be such an imbecile to believe that she returned your feelings?* No sudden bolt of love had struck her heart as it had his.

He sighed, pulling away his gaze with difficulty. He'd better return to the Folly. Later he'd send down the Latch twins to finish the work with the trestle tables. Even though they were dim-witted, the twins' carpentry skills were probably superior to his. He picked up his toolbox and left the shed. He threw a last glance at Marianne and was rewarded as she returned it. The air seemed to catch fire between them, and she jerked her head aside as if burned.

Not wholly untouched, he thought as pleasure filled his chest. Perhaps she wasn't as immune as she pretended to be. Still, she thought she was being bullied by a butler, and she would never admit her attraction to an unsuitable gentleman. If only he could reveal his true identity to Marianne . . . if only this charade was over, and the love letters destroyed.

Thinking about those letters, he entered the butler's pantry at the Folly. He washed off his face, inspected his false mustache, and rebound his wound. Attired in a black coat and faultless linen, he sneaked upstairs to the guest rooms. Someone had hidden the letters in the urn in the library, but who? He would systematically search every room until he found them. He'd start with Mrs. Caldway's bedchamber while she was by the pond feeding the swans.

Mrs. Caldway's room was shrouded in semidarkness. He pulled one set of blue velvet curtains carefully aside and began riffling through the tallboy in the corner. He stiffened as the surprise of a snore reached his ear. He glanced toward the half-open door to the dressing room. The maid! He'd better hurry. . . .

Unsavory business, he thought as he gingerly touched embroidered handkerchiefs and sheer nightgowns. Nervous, he listened to the maid snoring. What if she awakened and found him here? As quietly as he could, he went through the rest of the drawers and the escritoire. No letters to be found except one on the blotter that Mrs. Caldway was in the process of writing. He certainly wouldn't stoop to reading her personal mail. Grand-mother might have, had she been in his shoes. Thank God she wasn't. He glanced under the pillows and under the bed, behind flower arrangements and in the portman-teaus stacked on top of the carved walnut wardrobe. Nothing.

The maid's snores grew uneven, and after trumpeting like an elephant once, she coughed. The cot creaked, and Leith rushed to the door on soft feet. He drew a sigh of relief as he closed it quietly behind him. Phew, that was a close one. No luck this time, but surely he would find the letters in one of these guest rooms. Such sordid business! This was the last time Grandmother would bully him into acting out her wild schemes.

He glanced at the clock on the table in the hallway. He'd better make sure the silver was properly arranged in the dining room for the small dinner Lady Randome had planned for her relatives. Just a quiet gathering since the house was in deepest mourning. But if Leith wasn't mistaken, the finest china and silver would be used. Lady Randome liked to display her wealth.

He went into the dining room and noted that the maids had laid the table to perfection. He inspected the place cards and experienced a pleasurable jolt as he saw Marianne Darby's name on one of them.

Chapter Five

THE BUTLER RECEIVED MARIANNE AND MISS DEW AT the imposing double doors of the Folly at exactly seven o'clock that evening. Marianne blushed as she glanced at his solemn face. Only his eyes twinkled, and she relived the memory of their kiss with vivid clarity. The impudence of the man, she thought, startled, as he gave her an imperceptible wink. Really! She ought to inform Lady Randome of Sherry's shocking ways. At the same time she couldn't deny that she was flattered. Swinton Langley wanted her for her substantial dowry, and no other gentleman had shown his appreciation of her for herself, like Sherry. He surely didn't believe that he had a chance at her hand . . . or did he?

She gave him a scathing glance, but he was conversing with Miss Dew about the lovely evening sun as he led them to the salon where the family had gathered before dinner.

He bowed at her by the door. "Have you forgiven me, Miss Darby?" he whispered after Miss Dew had passed the threshold ahead of her niece.

"I don't know," Marianne said sternly, and unfurled her fan. She fluttered it in front of her face to cool off the rising blush. He ought to nip that grin off his countenance. "You look like you wouldn't mind repeating the crime," she added.

"Oh, Miss Darby, when was love ever a crime?" he whispered in shocked tones.

"It becomes a crime when propriety is not involved," Marianne said, and swept past him into the room. She could have sworn she heard a soft chuckle behind her as he closed the door.

Marianne didn't see him until dinner, when he was in the process of serving wine. She was seated between Mordecay Follett and young Virgil Fitzwilliam. She was soon bored listening to their conversation about the horse races and a cockfight scheduled in the neighboring village. Virgil Fitzwilliam must have noticed the small yawn behind her hand as he finally addressed her.

"Surely, Miss Darby, you must miss the season in London," he said. "I don't see how you can live in this isolated village without the mad whirl of routs and balls."

Hurt at the memory of her failure in London two years ago pinched Marianne's heart.

"Why, Miss Darby, you must not tarry in this godforsaken place until you're too old—" Mr. Fitzwilliam ended his faux pas with a bout of coughing, but the words had been said for everyone's benefit.

A long arm stretched around her. "More wine, Miss Darby," the butler asked, and she nodded. His presence added comfort against the young man's heartless comments.

"I don't mind living in a small village," she countered. "I have many interests that can't be indulged in town. Gardening for one."

She sensed the silent scoff from Mr. Fitzwilliam, and she turned to Mr. Follett on her other side. "You must miss your uncle very much. I'm sorry this is such a sad gathering."

"The old goat got his comeuppance at last," said the unfeeling Mr. Follett. "I haven't shed a tear."

Marianne gasped, shocked by such a heartless admission.

"A more miserable miser I have yet to meet," he continued, and Mr. Fitzwilliam agreed in no uncertain terms.

"Why, yes, Uncle was tightfisted. He would never lend us money in a tight spot. Not that we've ever been in one," he added, sending a glance at his formidable mother to see if she'd heard his conversation.

Marianne viewed Mrs. Fitzwilliam, who was sitting on the opposite side of the huge table, deeply engaged in conversation with Miss Dew.

"I have been in monetary difficulties more than once," said the tactless Mr. Follett. "I asked Uncle for five thousand pounds once, and he gave me *five*. He said that should teach me not to come to him with my gambling debts. What is a destitute gentleman to do, flee from his debtors?"

Not discuss your debts at the dinner table, thought Marianne, appalled at her partners' bad taste. "I'd say we need some rain. The wells are drying out," she said feebly.

"Surely not until after the funeral. There's nothing worse than getting one's feet wet and muddy," said Virgil Fitzwilliam with a shudder. "Might bring on one of my coughs. I have a weak chest, y'know. Always had.

Mother makes me drink vile potions if I as much as sneeze.''

The young man then made Marianne privy to his every ailment since his childhood, and she marveled that he was still alive to tell about them. According to him, he'd been at death's door more times than he could count. Marianne hid a huge yawn behind her napkin, wishing the arms of the tall clock in the corner would move faster.

Without thinking, she watched the handsome butler usher in the maids with the soup tureen and a platter of fish. He gave one of them, Lottie, the prettiest, one of his warm grins, and the fangs of jealousy bit down hard into Marianne's heart. Disgusted with herself for such a base reaction, she toyed with the fork beside her plate as her partners conversed over her head. If the butler were close enough, she would shove the prongs of her fork into his leg.

The thought cheered her considerably as the meal dragged on into eternity, it seemed. She was regaled with the tale of Mr. Follett's failed courtships, and she didn't blame the young ladies who had turned down his proposal. No lady in her right mind would marry anyone as selfish and heartless as Mr. Follett.

''One day you might find the lady of your heart,'' she said to encourage a cheerful ending to his woeful tale.

''She must be an heiress, or I will starve to death. The mountain of bills on my desk grows taller every day.'' His lips took a downward turn, and his face fell into an expression of gloom.

A trembling sob from the head of the table snared Marianne's attention. Lady Randome was wiping her eyes with her napkin. After the fish had been cleared away, she tapped her wineglass with her spoon. Everyone quieted and turned toward the old lady.

"It's not my place really to hold this speech. Nigel—my only son—should be here tonight." A trembling sigh wafted toward the listeners. "He should take his rightful place at the other end of the table, where Egbert's chair is now empty." She gave a long pause. "However, Nigel is serving his country in Spain, perhaps at this very moment risking his life to rid Europe of that mad dog Napoleon. Perhaps the message of his father's death has just reached him and he's without the comfort of his family. He might need me now. . . ." Her voice petered out, and Marianne wondered if the widow would be able to finish her speech.

Lady Randome somehow rallied and continued, "I'm grateful that you're here in my moment of sorrow, and tomorrow we'll lay to rest the head of this family. Then Nigel will be the master of this house and the Randome land. I'm sure Egbert provided well for all of—"

"Hah!" cried Mrs. Caldway. "He told me—in confidence—that everything was going to Nigel. We won't receive a penny of his money. Not that I care," she said in more subdued tones.

An uncomfortable silence stretched in the room, and Marianne fervently wished she were elsewhere. She coughed into her napkin to break the hostile spell. The old earl's sisters were here out of duty, not out of love. Mrs. Fitzwilliam and Mrs. Caldway exchanged speaking glances.

"Egbert was an unfeeling sort of man. He didn't care a fig what happened to his family," Mrs. Fitzwilliam said with a sniff. "Why, I have sometimes begged him—" Her lips closed over the rest of her words, and she shot uneasy glances around the room.

"He grew bitter with age," Mrs. Caldway filled in. "His temper tantrums frightened me sometimes." She raised her chin. "He certainly would never lend a helping hand in the time of crisis. I pray Nigel will be different."

Marianne doubted that Nigel, the new earl, would be a more generous soul than his father. She remembered him as a cold fish who looked down on anyone with a lesser title than viscount.

The rest of the meal was strained, and Marianne drew a sigh of relief when it was over. She followed the ladies to the door, where the butler met them, holding a silver salver. He looked grave, and Marianne realized he wasn't immune to the pall hanging over the mansion.

"Lady Randome," he said. "A messenger just left." He held out the tray toward the dowager, who took the official-looking letter with clawlike fingers. "Who is it from?" she asked peevishly.

"I'm afraid it's from the War Office."

Marianne gasped, sensing more bad news.

The gentlemen joined the ladies in the hallway. "Perhaps it's a note of condolence," said Virgil Fitzwilliam.

Lady Randome tore open the seal and unfolded the stiff missive. She read the message, then fell into a swoon. Sherry was there to catch her as she fainted.

Mrs. Fitzwilliam snatched the paper from Lady Randome's nerveless fingers. She moaned out loud and clutched her hand to her heart.

"Nigel is dead," she croaked. "He was shot as he carried a bulletin from one of the camps to the headquarters."

Shocked silence fell as everyone stared at each other,

as if seeking reaffirmation that the world wasn't going mad.

Mrs. Caldway put her arm around Mrs. Fitzwilliam, and Virgil propped up Mordecay Follett, who seemed to be on the verge of fainting.

Miss Dew whispered to Marianne that they ought to help Lady Randome to her room and keep a vigil all night. The old lady might die from the shock of two deaths so closely together. Marianne watched as Sherry waved his handkerchief in front of Lady Randome's face after lifting her onto the hard settle by the front door.

"Well, well, this means that Mordecay is now the Earl of Randome, doesn't it, old fellow?" said Virgil, slapping his cousin's back. "Surely life changes quickly, don't you think? One day poor, the next day wealthy beyond measure. I hope you'll remember your friends in their time of difficulty."

Marianne thought she saw a smile of satisfaction on Virgil's face, and she disliked him more for it. She exchanged a glance with Sherry, and she could have sworn he wore an expression of—relief? How odd, to be sure . . . Why would he be relieved that Mordecay Follett was now the Earl of Randome?

Leith *was* relieved. If Follett had sent the blackmail notes to Grandmother, it now meant he would stop pressing her for funds. As a wealthy man, he didn't need Grandmother's five thousand pounds. Still, Leith had to find the love letters and destroy them. Then another situation like this would not crop up, and he wouldn't have to don a false mustache and eyeglasses that dimmed his vision.

"Miss Darby, would you help me with Lady Randome," he asked with authority. He delegated two maids to arrange Lady Randome's bed and sent a footman with a message to Reverend Otterby. The reverend would have to include Nigel in his funeral service tomorrow.

Momentarily he forgot that he was naught but a butler and ordered the servants around in a stentorian voice, as if he was the lord of the manor. Miss Darby gave him a glance full of suspicion and he lowered his gaze, taking on a more humble mien. Between them, they led Lady Randome, who had finally come to, up the stairs to her bedchamber. She was in a sad state, and Marianne asked the butler to have the doctor summoned.

Leith couldn't believe his ears as he heard Lady Randome say, "I wonder what happened to those love letters. What a humiliation that proof of Egbert's faithlessness has come to light. I'm ruined," she muttered to herself, and began to cry in earnest.

The doctor arrived in haste as Lady Randome's maid and Marianne were putting her to bed. He sedated her, and Marianne waited by the bedside until the frail old lady had fallen asleep. Lady Randome had always been a good friend to her, and her spirits plummeted as she shared the widow's sorrow. The old lady had lost her husband, and now her son. . . . Marianne wondered what the future would be like for the Randomes with the new earl, Mordecay, at the helm.

Chapter Six

LEITH THOUGHT ABOUT THE WORDS THAT LADY RAN-dome had uttered about the love letters. Perhaps the blackmailer who had lost the letters thought they still were with the corpse. Since the servants had been talking about the letters at the time of their first sensational appearance, everyone knew about their erstwhile resting spot in the dead earl's hand. *Only I and Miss Darby know that the letters are no longer there.* Perhaps the extortionist would come in search of the letters tonight when everyone slept. He had kept vigil last night, but no one had entered the room. The villain might be a wily old fox, thinking no one would observe his moves, but Leith would be more cunning. He ought to stand guard in the parlor one more night, just in case. He wished he could lay his hands on those epistles and be done with the charade.

Where were the letters? Had Mrs. Caldway known they were in the urn all along? Did she know their whereabouts right now? Was Virgil Fitzwilliam a scoundrel with huge gambling debts—like Mordecay Follett?

Was Mrs. Fitzwilliam a grasping old widow? He had no answers to those questions.

He pulled off the ill-fitting eyeglasses that irritated the tender flesh behind his ears, and tossed them on the table in the butler's pantry. The skin itched under his mustache, but he didn't dare to pull it off lest someone summoned him upstairs. He chafed under the restrictions his new employment placed upon him.

He wanted to go courting at Marianne's door as the Honorable Leith Sheridan, not as the ramshackle butler Lester Sherry. He abhorred the subterfuge now that Miss Darby—the woman he'd searched for since he matured to manhood—had entered his life. Besides, he wasn't a very good butler, and Marianne had discovered that in a trice. It might only be a matter of time before she would tear his mustache off and denounce him as an impostor.

The evening settled in every corner of the mansion. Darkness came, and as Leith made the rounds to extinguish any burning candles and check the doors, he noticed that Virgil Fitzwilliam—that coxcomb—and the new earl, Follett, were smoking cheroots on the terrace and drinking brandy. Probably celebrating Follett's new status . . .

"Sherry, come here, old fellow," called the new Lord Randome.

Leith narrowed his gaze, noticing the open door to the parlor where the old earl's corpse lay in state. He bowed. "You're wishing, my lord?"

"Bring us some more brandy, there's a good fellow." As Leith nodded and returned toward the house the earl added, "By the way, how is Lady Randome?"

"The doctor sedated her, my lord. He said she should be resting until the funeral. Miss Darby and Miss Dew are at her side at the moment."

"A most dutiful and dull woman that Miss Darby,"

said Mordecay under his breath. "A veritable country bumpkin. Had nothing to say for herself at dinner. No wonder she can't find a gentleman to wed her, what with that ugly limp of hers and her lack of conversation. I can't say I blame the fellows for giving her a wide berth. She'll remain on the shelf indefinitely."

"You're right there," said Virgil Fitzwilliam. "Not my type at all, but I hear she brings a substantial dowry." He glanced at Leith. "What are you staring at? Fetch the brandy, man!"

Leith burned with wrath. He took a step toward the smiling cad, his hands bunched into fists as he was about to defend his beloved. At the last moment he recalled his station and stood motionless on the flagstones. "Certainly, my lord," he forced out between clenched teeth. Turning around abruptly, he hurried into the house before he did something foolish.

When he'd delivered the brandy, Leith sneaked into the empty library at one end of the terrace and, concealed behind the curtain, listened to the two men's conversation. Perhaps it would yield some information about the letters. To his chagrin, the men spoke of nothing but the horse races and the favors of a certain bird of paradise in London.

An hour later Fitzwilliam excused himself and went upstairs for the night. Mordecay sat down in a wooden lawn chair and cradled the brandy bottle in the crook of his arm while sipping from his glass. Was he going to sit there all night? Since he had gained unexpected wealth, he would surely stop the blackmailing scheme against Grandmother—*if* he was the culprit. He certainly wouldn't need the letters now. *I will search the rest of the bedchambers as soon as I get a chance.* Leith yawned, his limbs weighed down with fatigue. Last night's vigil was taking its toll.

With another yawn, he lifted his face toward the dark sky outside. He felt the tension in the air, the leaden pressure of a building storm. He worried about Marianne. Would she return home in bad weather, or would she remain overnight? That last possibility cheered him, and he prayed the thunderstorm would be particularly heavy.

He went to the door on quiet feet. Better leave the new earl to his brandy bottle and not interfere. Leith itched to tell him a few choice words to avenge sweet Marianne, but at this juncture it was beyond his station to intervene on her behalf. He heard steps along the flagstones outside and halted his progress to see who was taking air.

He peered around the curtain, and to his amazement, he saw Marianne standing in the darkness, her face turned toward the sky. Her white high-waisted dress acted as a soft beacon as light spilled from one of the windows above and touched the silky material. He couldn't see her expression, but his heart started to beat faster.

"Who goes there?" slurred Mordecay from the depths of his chair.

"Miss Darby. I needed to take a walk. The air is close tonight. Gathering itself toward a storm, I'll warrant."

"Hrmph," snorted Mordecay, and heaved himself upright. "I thought—hic—you would keep vigil at my aunt's—hic—bed tonight. Most saintly of you."

"Her abigail is with her, but I will stay overnight just in case she asks for me." She sounded uncertain, worried. "I hope I don't intrude on your sorrow."

He staggered toward her, and Leith squeezed the edge

of the velvet drapes in anger. What was going through the scoundrel's head?

"I'm sure—hic—I don't mind." He burped and stood swaying on the terrace, only two steps from Marianne.

"Lady Randome might wake up, and she needs to know that she has friends around her at a sorrowful time like this."

"Sorrowful? It was about time the old—hic—goat stuck his spoon in the wall, and that blasted Nigel as well." As Marianne took a startled step back he moved closer to her. "I say, would you mind—hic—terribly keeping vigil by my bed, or rather *in* it?"

Marianne gasped and wrapped her arms around herself as if to protect herself from the horror of his suggestion. She turned to flee inside, but Mordecay got a grip on her elbow and tugged her toward his chest. She lost her balance, and if Mordecay's hand hadn't gripped the curve of her hip, she would have fallen.

A hot haze of fury filled Leith as he watched Mordecay's tactics. The man wasn't only a cad, he was a libertine of the first order. So as not to show his fury, Leith moved with controlled steps, his back stiff, his arms loosely at his side.

"Miss Darby?" he inquired. Any pretext would do to distract the earl. "Did you ask for a glass of lemonade, or did I get the message wrong?" He glanced at Mordecay as if he could punch his face, but quickly lowered his gaze so that the young earl wouldn't notice his hostility. Soon enough he would get his revenge, and then the earl would go to bed with—not one—but *two* shiners. The man deserved to be called out. . . .

Marianne looked pale and apprehensive. Mordecay lurched sideways and finally dropped his hold on her arm.

"Y-yes," she stammered. "I do wish you would bring a glass. In fact, I think I'll return inside with you, Sherry." She hastened to his side, and he bowed, letting her enter before him.

"Dashed nuisance that—hic—you should come right now, Sherry. Damned bad timing." Mordecay crashed back into his chair, and when it overturned, Leith didn't take one step to help him up. "I want my servants to have—hic—impeccable timing."

"He was forcing himself on you, Miss Darby," said Leith as he held the library door for her.

She nodded, pressing her handkerchief to the corner of her eye. "He was very crude." She went into the vast hallway. "I'll be in the rose salon. Please bring the lemonade there."

"I could draw and quarter him," Leith muttered as he hurried to the kitchen for a pitcher of lemonade that the cook had made earlier and placed in the cellar to cool.

He returned, opening the door softly. She stood by the open window, staring into the darkness. A single candle glowed on the mantelpiece, and the rest of the room was filled with shadows. She looked tired and sad as he pressed a glass of the cool beverage in her hand.

"This ought to make you feel better." He wanted to wrap his arms around her, but couldn't find the courage to do so. She would only reject him—be outraged and accuse him of being just like the earl.

"Mr. Sherry, perhaps I shouldn't talk to you like this . . . but I feel as if . . . as if I know you now. After this morning, I mean." Her voice trembled on the last words. "I heard their conversation, you know."

He almost forgot himself and told her he'd overheard the men speak, too, but only cleared his throat and said, "Conversation, miss?"

She nodded. "They—Mr. Fitzwilliam and Mr. Follett were discussing me on the terrace, and Lady Randome's window was open. It's right above the library. They called me dull and other epithets." Her hand and handkerchief blurred up to her eyes, then fell down to her side. "I know I'm not popular with the gentlemen due to my limp, but I'm not *dull*," she said with much feeling.

"I don't think I'm the only man who finds you wholly adorable," he said softly. "You must have scores of admirers." Still he didn't dare to move toward her lest she take flight. The rude earl had frightened her too much as it was. "I didn't realize you had a limp, Miss Darby, I thought it was a natural part of your walk."

She flinched and gave him a long, hard stare. "Don't lie to my face, Mr. Sherry." She drew a deep breath. "Do you want to know how it happened?"

He was sure she wouldn't talk like this to him if the circumstances had been different. "If you want to tell me about it," he said quietly, and folded his hands behind his back.

"Mother died three years ago, and I miss her sorely. But Miss Dew is like a second mother to me, always has been. Father, a bluff gentleman—well, you'll understand if you ever meet him—only has eyes for his horses and foals." She gave a tremulous smile.

"You like horses as well, Miss Darby, don't you?"

"Of course I do, always did. Anyway, that fateful day in my childhood, a cat had a litter of kittens in the stables. Up in the hayloft. I climbed up to play with the little ones, and when I stepped down the ladder, I lost my balance and fell. You see, I broke my hip and it didn't mend properly."

"It wasn't such a tragedy, surely?" he asked softly. "You could have broken your neck."

"Yes!" she said with a flare of temper. "But that *dashed* fall ruined my chances at finding a suitable husband later. Don't you see? Follett and Fitzwilliam were right. No one wants to marry me because of that physical flaw. I went to London and suffered through a season, returning without an offer. Not even the fortune hunters were interested in me. I was a country bumpkin visiting London, and I couldn't force myself into the mold of a sophisticated debutante. There are more things to life than lovely dresses and balls," she spat with such vehemence that Leith took a step back.

He nodded, but before he could say anything to verify her observations, she continued, "There are horses, birds, bird nests and eggs, nodding bluebells, the changing of the seasons, kittens, fresh milk that's still warm, blue skies, grass swaying in the summer breeze . . . etcetera."

Leith chuckled. "I can understand why you found the social whirl shallow and pointless."

"Do you raise your nose at such countrified pleasures, Mr. Sherry? After all, you're a highly elevated servant who has spent time in the wealthy aristocratic households of the metropolis."

"Yes, I've lived in London . . . but I can see the merits of horse riding on a dewy morning, admiring the wildflowers in the meadows, fishing for trout in a glittering stream. I don't mind any of that." He thought for a moment, then said, "Yet London has its allure, too, perhaps a side you never experienced in your short season there. Horse riding in the Rotten Row, picnics at Sadler's Wells and Richmond Park, the theater, the opera, the artists and poets."

"You sound like you know awfully much about the life of an aristocrat."

He nodded, careful to school his face into a neutral

smile. "I have served aristocrats, yes. I know the routine. *I,* however, would like to share my pleasures with you, Miss Darby, be they in a meadow or at a bazaar in London."

Marianne took a step back as if warding him off. "You're not going to start with that piece of nonsense again, Mr. Sherry. Flattering me, I mean."

He shrugged. "I know it was terribly wrong of me to kiss you this morning, but I meant every word I said then. Unlike the new earl, I will not force myself on you." He took a deep breath. "If it were permissible, I would court you properly. . . ."

His voice trailed off, as he didn't want to explain about his charade. She must find it unbelievably forward of him to mention courtship. Oh, he longed to smooth her untidy hair back, calm her, and assure her that in his eyes, she was perfect just as she was.

"I truly didn't know that you had a weak hip," he said earnestly. "I thought your gait had a quirky personal touch, a quite endearing detail."

She laughed, a hollow sound tinged with doubt. "That's a plumper if I ever heard one. I—everyone knows I limp, and no gentleman wants a less-then-perfect wife."

"Are they afraid you would pass it on to your children?" he asked with a hint of a smile in his voice. How could such a lovely, such a vibrant young lady worry so about a minor flaw that lent her distinction? He couldn't understand it.

"No need to wax sarcastic, Sherry." Marianne watched him closely to see if he was mocking her, but no contempt curled on his lips. He confused her with his kindness, his self-confidence and lack of servility. It was easy to forget that he was a butler, but reality always jolted her back. She ought not to be here, yet she couldn't bring herself to move. His presence soothed her.

"You cannot place your failure in London on one small flaw like that," he said.

"No . . . My mind knows better than that," she said, trying to belittle the feeling of growing intimacy between them. The circumstances had brought them together. "But my self-confidence does not improve with that knowledge. However, I'm not stupid, nor am I dull."

"That's right. You shouldn't listen to words from the mouths of imbeciles. I shouldn't talk ill of my employer, but the new earl is touched in his upper works. His head is mostly filled with sawdust. He and Mr. Fitzwilliam are birds of a feather."

She chuckled, and tears glistened on her eyelashes. "You're incorrigible, Sherry. If they knew what you've done today, first kissing me most shockingly, then scorning the intelligence of your betters, they would throw you out on your ear."

He laughed, wishing he could rip off his mustache and kiss her silly. "I have been told on various occasions that I have a big mouth. Perhaps it will be my downfall." He took a step toward her. "A voice inside is urging me to kiss you again, Miss Darby, but I won't listen to it—not unless you want me to."

"Certainly not!" she said in shocked tones. "I should not be closeted here with you. It's just that—"

He moved a step closer. "Yes?" He could smell the light floral scent of her hair, and every time he inhaled the fragrance, he seemed to lose all coherent thought. Golden tendrils floated on her shoulders, giving her an air of vulnerability.

She waved her hand weakly in dismissal. "I . . . I

don't know what I'm saying.'' She gulped some lemonade, then set the glass down resolutely on an Oriental table by the window. He blew lightly at the wisps of hair at the nape of her slender neck and wondered how her skin would taste. Perhaps better than strawberries and cream, his favorite dessert. He leaned forward, drawn against his better judgment to sample the creamy skin.

She jerked aside as if sensing his plan. ''I must go now!'' Yet she stood there, poised as a doe scenting danger.

He straightened, arranging his face into a neutral smile. ''Lady Randome won't awaken until tomorrow. You must be very tired. Do you want me to escort you home?''

She shook her head. ''I promised Lady Randome I would stay.'' She sighed deeply, as if thinking of the bleak night ahead.

''I take it you get lonely at times here in Spiggott Hollow.''

She smiled. ''Not very often, but yes, sometimes. Besides the new head gardener here at the Folly, you're the first stranger who has moved here in many years.'' She gave him a steady glance with those incredible blue-green eyes, reducing him to an incoherent fool.

''Needless to say,'' she continued, ''we don't encounter many eligible gentlemen in Spiggott Hollow.''

''They don't know what treasure they are missing in you, Miss Darby.'' He took a step closer to her.

She pushed him in the chest. ''Stop it, Sherry. I don't want to hear any more of your glib lies. If you think I will fall for you because I don't have someone else—except Swinton Langley, of course—you're sadly mistaken.''

''I'm not teasing you, or hoping to find you an easy conquest, Miss Darby. I'm serious in my admiration.''

She rushed toward the door, and he moved to follow her, but he realized that she'd had enough attention from him for one night. If she wasn't such a sweet and lonely lady, she would never listen to his blandishments. How would he convince her that he was serious?

She sprinted up the stairs to the bedrooms above, and Leith watched her from the doorway. At last the house was silent, except for a distant crashing of thunder. The hallway lay in deep shadows, and he decided to take his rest on his narrow cot in the butler's pantry.

A moving shadow by the door leading to the room with the corpse alerted his attention.

Chapter Seven

THEN TWO THINGS HAPPENED AT ONCE. THE SNORTING of horses and the shouting of a coachman sounded outside, and Miss Darby returned to the top of the stairs. "Who is that, arriving so late?"

Leith made a dash for the black shadow, but it had rushed through the room with the corpse, then disappeared through the French doors leading to the terrace. Dashed nuisance! He had no time to brood over the identity of the shadow, as other pressing matters needed his attention. What was on Marianne's mind as she returned downstairs, and who had arrived at this late hour?

"Sherry?" Marianne called out. "Are you there? I saw a carriage coming up the drive. Are you expecting more guests for the funeral?" She peered into the darkness below and watched as the butler lit the candles in the wall sconces by the door.

"I don't know, Miss Darby, but I will investigate. Lady Randome said nothing about visitors."

Marianne admired his powerful stride as he walked

across the white-and-black-checkered marble floor toward the entrance. She chided herself for confiding in him earlier. She must have lost her mind to speak so openly to a veriest stranger. Fact is, he didn't feel like a stranger, nor was she threatened by him as she was by other gentlemen she had encountered.

Swinton Langley didn't threaten her, but she'd known him all her life. She didn't love him, nor did he love her. Not that it mattered in matrimony, but to her it mattered. She would have to squelch Swinton's increasingly amorous attitude. He had his eyes on her dowry, nothing else. That fact didn't bother her so much as the thought of spending the rest of her life being married to Swinton and his *mother*. It was not to be borne.

Sherry had shaken her so much with his attention that nothing would be the same again. He'd touched some longing in her that now was demanding to be satisfied.

The pounding increased just as Sherry opened the stately double doors, then stopped just as abruptly.

She could hear a demanding female voice coming from the outside. "Aunt Fulvia, let the flunkies carry in the luggage. I, for one, am so tired I can barely carry my own reticule."

When Marianne heard that the visitors to the Folly were ladies, she stepped across the hallway. She reached the door just as the butler spoke.

"Vivian?" Sherry asked in a strange voice. Marianne glanced at him sharply. He knew the lady, was on a first-name basis with her.

"Leith?" The young woman stopped on the threshold, staring with amazement at the butler.

Sherry stepped forward, bowing deferentially. "No . . . you have my identity mixed up with that of a footman at my former employment in town. Lester

Sherry, at your service. Miss Vivian Worton, is it not?''

The young lady's eyes widened, and she clapped a begloved hand to her mouth. "Sherry?''

The butler hurried forward and Marianne noticed the whispered exchange that happened between the two people. An odd circumstance, as if Sherry and the lady were old friends, perhaps even . . . *intimates.* A chill crawled up Marianne's spine as that unladylike word rose in her mind. Sherry indulged in the sport of seducing ladies. How many fair heads had he turned with his blandishments?

Anger stormed through her, but she kept her temper at bay. Miss Vivian Worton stepped inside and Marianne saw immediately that she was a lady of quality, dressed in the first stare. She stood a regal five feet and (possibly) ten inches above the floor. She was almost as tall as Sherry, and she could afford to look down her imperious nose at the world. She did now, but Marianne did not read any malice in Miss Worton's dark eyes, only hauteur.

"And who are you? I expected Cousin Egbert's wife to welcome us—even though the hour is late.''

Marianne introduced herself. "I'm afraid lady Randome is asleep at this time. Have you come to attend Lord Randome's funeral?''

"Yes, he was my dear father's cousin, so I must show my respects—with Aunt Fulvia in attendance, of course.''

"Oh, you must be of the Yorkshire Wortons. I heard Lady Randome speak of you.''

"Did you travel from London today, Miss Worton?'' inquired Sherry.

A rather too familiar question, Marianne thought—for a butler to a lady of quality.

"Lei—Sherry—I . . . what . . ." Miss Worton's words seemed to get stuck in her throat, and Marianne studied her closely. Miss Worton was pulling at the fingertips of her kid gloves, for a moment losing her regal composure.

"I'll wake a footman to help with the luggage," Sherry said.

A thunderclap shook the beams of the house and gusts of wind rattled the trees. Rain started pouring down outside.

Marianne glanced at Sherry as he wended his way around her and Miss Worton. He didn't meet her gaze. A deep frown etched his forehead, and she sensed that he was very upset. It would be upsetting to have one's lover arrive as one was working on another conquest. . . . Dashed scoundrel! She would take the first opportunity to wring his miserable neck.

Miss Worton followed him inside, and as Marianne decided to do the same she was interrupted by a querulous voice coming from the interior of the carriage. Aunt Fulvia, no doubt.

"Is no one going to help me out of this bone-jarring vehicle?" she asked, and Marianne went out into the rain and stuck her head inside the traveling chaise. Given the circumstances, it wasn't odd that the butler had completely forgotten the old lady. He only had eyes for the regal Miss Worton with her elegant silk pelisse and fashionable hat.

Marianne helped the old lady inside. The tiny black-clad individual with wiry gray hair and watery blue eyes shook out her skirts, drops of water scattering on the marble floor.

"Vivian doesn't like funerals. I don't understand why in the world she insisted on coming down to this godforsaken part of the country to attend the funeral of some distant relative. She's harebrained; I make no bones about that.''

Marianne watched as Sherry conversed agitatedly with Miss Worton at the bottom of the staircase. She heard a few words like ''hiding'' . . . ''run away'' . . . ''wit's end.'' She wished fervently she could hear their muttered discussion in its entirety.

Leith glowered at Vivian and longed to shake her.

''I was *bored* to flinders in London once you disappeared, Leith. I finally managed to milk the information of your whereabouts from your grandmother. I wager she felt guilty for keeping a betrothed couple apart for so long. So here I am,'' Vivian hissed. ''Whether you like it or not.''

''What can I say?'' countered Leith. ''As long as you keep mum about my real identity, I don't have any objection to your being here.'' He slanted a glance at Marianne, realizing that he cared more for her than he would ever care for Vivian. What a pickle! It had been the wrong move to offer for Vivian just to keep her safe, and to keep an old promise that had been made between their fathers. Still, it wasn't Vivian's fault that he was embroiled in one of Grandmother's wild schemes.

''How could you sink so low, Leith, to act as a butler! I don't approve of your guise. It's shameful, and hideous! Lady Longford did not explain why you're here, and why you're playacting at being a butler. Does it involve one of your wild wagers?'' She turned around, her chin decidedly pugnacious. ''If I'm to keep silent about your identity, you must explain *everything*. It's the least you can do.''

Leith abhorred the very idea of confiding in his

fiancée. She was a notorious gossip, and anything he told her would slip out in a conversation whether she planned to let it slip or not. She could not keep anything inside, so he always avoided telling her anything that was important and private. But the real problem here was whether Marianne had overheard Vivian call him Leith. How would he explain that if she asked him?

"I shall tell you everything in the morning, Vivian. You *must* keep quiet about this, remember that."

"I'll be made a laughingstock if this ever comes out," she said with a sniff. "I won't say a word."

"Very well," he said, in a softer tone. "You must be exhausted after your trip." He glanced around. "Where's your abigail?"

"She was snoring in the coach as we arrived, and probably still is."

"I shall fetch her and see to it that you get a cup of cocoa sent up to your room." He set off, but Vivian grabbed his arm. From the corner of his eye, he noticed Marianne's suspicious expression. Her anger literally rolled in waves toward him.

"Leith, before I leave from here, I want us to decide on a date for the wedding. I'm displeased that you're always inventing excuses." She gave him a hard stare. "I know I had to be in mourning for a year after dearest Mama died, but that year is long gone. Surely . . . ?"

A twinge of guilt stole through Leith. He'd been unfair with Vivian, but if he were honest with himself, he couldn't think of a more daunting event than facing his formidable fiancée at the altar of St. George's in Hanover Square. Shackled for life to a woman who would try to regulate his every step. Not that he would accept that, but she would resent any disobedience on his part and devote herself to making his life miserable.

"Yes, of course we must discuss the matter," he said noncommittally and fled outside to find the abigail.

The old lady leaned on Marianne's arm, and they joined Miss Worton, who—with smoldering eyes—watched Leith disappear.

"I take it you knew Mr. Sherry in his past employment?" Marianne asked, angry with herself for feeling jealous of the young lady who evidently had Sherry's ear. The butler was a veritable Don Juan, no mistake about that.

"Well . . . yes." Miss Worton pulled off her gloves and slapped them against the palm of her hand. "Could you please show us to our rooms, Miss Darby? We would prefer two connecting chambers since we're sharing one maid."

"Sherry?" said Aunt Fulvia, and peered nearsightedly into the pouring rain outside. "What a strange *frivolous* name for a servant, don't you think? Next one will hear the name 'Whiskey,' or 'Claret.' Hmmph! How come you're on speaking terms with a butler, Vivian?"

"I . . . ahem, well, not really on speaking terms, Aunt Fulvia. I asked him about the funeral arrangements, that's all."

Marianne stared at Miss Worton from between her eyelashes. The young lady was lying, that much was clear. Something very suspicious was going on between the butler and the lady. Marianne tucked that thought into her memory and decided she would never speak with Sherry again.

The funeral procession left the Folly at exactly half past ten in the morning, the crepe-draped hearse drawn by four black horses with nodding black plumes attached to their harnesses.

Marianne and Miss Dew, who had hurried home to change for the service and collect Squire Darby, joined the heavily veiled Lady Random in the churchyard. She leaned ponderously on Mrs. Fitzwilliam and Mrs. Caldway as she walked into the solemn stillness of the church. Miss Worton followed with Aunt Fulvia. The Randomes sat in the foremost pew, where generations of Randomes had sat before them, and the Darbys one pew behind.

As Marianne stepped in she noticed the impudent butler standing beside the stone steps, but she refused to acknowledge his presence. He would no doubt sit beside the other servants at the back of the church. The thought made her realize that her impossible infatuation with him was a terrible mistake. Father, who was a proud man, would never condone her liaison with a butler.

Squire Darby led her into the church on his arm. "Did you see that young man beside the steps?" he muttered. "The new Random butler, I presume."

Marianne nodded, keeping her face averted lest her vigilant father read the guilt in her expression.

"I could have sworn he was *staring* at you as if ready to eat you alive, Marianne. Did you know that?"

Marianne shook her head vehemently. "You must be mistaken, Papa. I don't know the fellow."

"You've spent quite some time with Lady Random, but I can understand your concern. She has received a double blow, and it's kind of you to console her in her sorrow." He took his seat, nodding stiffly to friends and acquaintances in the other pews. Marianne sat beside him, fingering her book of psalms. More was coming, perhaps a rebuke, she mused.

"Swinton, however, is displeased with your absences from home two mornings in a row. He pays his visits faithfully, and this morning he officially asked for your hand in marriage.''

Marianne gasped and gripped the hard wooden seat. ''Papa, we would never suit.''

''I've told you before that I will abide by your decision, even though I could *force* you to accept the fellow's proposal.''

Marianne met his shrewd sideways glance. ''I'm afraid not many suitors are beating down the door at Darby House. I advise you most strongly to accept his offer, Marianne. You won't be living far from home, and I look forward to dandling a grandchild on my knee in the near future. Hopefully the firstborn will be a boy, who I can teach to ride in due course.''

''Papa, Swinton's mother—''

''Shh, the service will be starting in a moment.''

So much for that discussion. *Papa says he abides by my decision, but he's already made it for me.* Marianne stifled an urge to flee outside. She was trapped. If she didn't accept Swinton, she would never be married, and her father would be displeased with her. The thought of remaining spouseless frightened her. She would very much like to have a family of her own, five, six children at least. But the thought of being surrounded by six squalling children bearing the imprint of Swinton Langley upon their faces was too much. Marianne hid her face in her handkerchief to smother a nervous chuckle. Several faces turned toward her with pity—as she grieved for the old earl.

When she left the church on her father's arm after the services, she convinced him to accompany her to her mother's grave. He reluctantly agreed, but when they approached the headstone, he found an excuse to greet an old friend strolling nearby. The two old gentlemen sat down on a bench under an oak tree, their backs turned toward Marianne.

She watered the wilting flowers, and suddenly she sensed a movement right beside her. Her head jerked up, and she gazed deeply into the blue, blue eyes of the Randome butler. "Oh, it's you," she blurted out, and the anger from the previous evening returned.

"I had to see you this morning and make sure that Mr. Fitzwilliam's wounding words didn't leave any scar on you."

"I was an utter fool to listen to you, and to unburden my problems, Mr. Sherry. Please disregard anything I said." She turned her rigid back toward him. "Now leave."

"Are you angry with me?" he asked softly. "Why?"

"If you don't know why, then don't expect me to explain it to you," she sputtered, in her agitation tilting the water can, so that water splattered all over the sandy lane and his highly polished shoes.

"I thought we were friends."

She couldn't help but look at him as his soft voice insinuated itself on her senses. Oh, what a slippery snake! "Friends with you? You have a very high opinion of yourself, Mr. Sherry. I was filled with sorrow last night, and you happened to lend a willing ear. I didn't care who listened to my woes."

He looked handsome and secure, even though his spectacles looked as if they pinched his nose terribly. He wore an immaculate black coat and a black armband around his upper arm. Hat in hand, he waited patiently for her to spill out the last of her wrath.

"The whole discussion was a mistake," she added as her heart slammed painfully against her ribs. If only he'd been old and bent, not tall and broad-shouldered, with the bluest, merriest eyes and the most sensitive lips a lady could wish for. If only old Boggs still worked at Randome's Folly, not this Adonis who made a conquest every time he stepped into the path of a young lady. Wed or unwed, it didn't seem to matter to him.

"I don't think it was a mistake," he said, much too kindly. "I believe there's a very special rapport between us, and don't deny it, Miss Darby. Don't deny your heart."

"As you have a special rapport with every susceptible female that crosses your path."

"I don't know—"

"Don't play innocent with me! You evidently filled Miss Worton's ear with the same flummery as you filled mine."

"That is a shocking misconception, Miss Darby. I have no idea—"

"If you don't stop this nonsense this very minute, I shall tell my father about you. He won't take any poppycock from you."

Sherry glanced at the squire, but the threat evidently didn't frighten him. "I can tell who gave you that stubborn chin," he said with a chuckle.

"Are you never serious, Mr. Sherry?" When he didn't answer, she continued, "You must think of me as an easy conquest, but I assure you, this is the last time I speak with you." She brushed off her black dress and gave him a scathing look. "In fact, next time I see you, I shall be betrothed."

He did look startled at that information. His eyes darkened, and a muscle twitched in his jaw. "That is most disturbing news. You mustn't marry—"

"Really, Mr. Sherry. A good butler would now be at the Folly supervising the serving of refreshments for the mourners."

"You very well know, Miss Darby, that 'butlering' is not one of my strong points." He rolled the brim of his hat between his hands, his only outer sign of agitation.

"Well, be grateful that I reminded you of your duties. Good day." She strode off, and to her disbelief, she heard him call her by her first name.

"Marianne, don't go—"

The squire looked up sharply, staring at the butler with ill-concealed contempt. He rose and went to meet Marianne on the path.

Marianne . . . A sweetness curled through her as Sherry took her name on his tongue, but she resolutely squelched the feeling. He had more tricks than she could count. Don Juans like him took to seduction like a calling. They wholly devoted their lives to bring about the downfall of respectable ladies. Not her, anyway. Not her. With a last glower at his crestfallen face (an expression that he must have practiced before the mirror for hours), she joined her father.

"I shall send a note to Swinton this afternoon, Papa," she said as they headed toward the Folly and the reception, "and ask him to call on me."

"I'm glad you've taken my advice. I didn't care much for the way the Randome butler was looking at you, and calling after you. I believe I ought to have a word with the new earl about him."

Marianne couldn't bear the thought of never seeing Sherry again. She clutched her father's arm. "Don't do that. The Randome domestic staff is none of our business. The butler means nothing to me, and he knows it. He converses with everyone equally."

"Hmm, one more ogle from him, and I shall see him dismissed."

Chapter Eight

SWINTON LANGLEY ARRIVED FIVE DAYS LATER AT Darby House with a new bounce in his step. An invitation to dinner with the family could only mean one thing: Marianne was accepting his suit. He would have her at last, but most important, he would have the sublime comfort of her dowry. Dearest Marianne . . .

Marianne regretted her foolishness in sending the dinner invitation to Swinton. After her argument with Sherry, she had longed to show him that she had other admirers besides him, *eligible* admirers. She had wanted to get back at the impossible butler, but instead she'd only put herself in a difficult situation. Sherry wouldn't be here to witness her admirer's overtures, and Swinton would press his suit with renewed determination, most likely try to persuade her that a speedy betrothal was of the essence.

She hadn't accepted him formally, but if she knew Swinton right, he had, in his mind, already met her at the altar and moved her into his house. A perfect companion for his mother as the old lady went through the trials and tribulations of her imagined ills. Of those there were many, and Marianne condemned herself for even momentarily believing she could spite the Randome butler with her attachment to Swinton Langley.

When Swinton—after a stultifying dinner—heard that she was going shopping on the morrow, he eagerly offered to escort her. "We must look at new things for my—our—house at the Ashford shops," he suggested with a meaningful smile at Marianne. "New drapes perhaps? And the rugs are somewhat threadbare in the drawing room."

Marianne didn't know what to answer. Her father took his cue as Swinton stared pointedly at him. "I shall retire to the study with a bottle. If you want to join me there *later,* Swinton, I'll serve you a glass. I have some excellent port put aside for an occasion like this."

Miss Dew rose from the table and invented a pressing matter that had to be attended to immediately. She threw a worried glance at Marianne as she left the dining room.

Marianne knew the awkward moment had come when she would have to speak with Swinton in private. She walked ahead of him into the adjoining parlor with its green-striped sofa and waited uncertainly in the middle of the floor.

"Miss Marianne, this is the happiest moment of my life, but also the most terrifying moment for an inveterate bachelor like me. Mother's health has prevented me from speaking—"

"I know you're wholly dedicated to the welfare of your mother, Swinton. It does you credit," Marianne interrupted to stall his proposal.

He seemed to lose the thread of his speech and repeatedly adjusted the shirt cuffs protruding from the sleeves of a particularly hideous coat of muddy brown satin. The corner of his left eye started to twitch, and Marianne said, "Perhaps we should join Miss Dew in the drawing room without delay."

"Oh . . . *no*. Can't do that, not yet." He suddenly sank down on one knee in front of her and took her hands in a clammy grip. She thought she heard a seam burst somewhere on his clothing, and she could barely suppress a nervous giggle. This is ridiculous! she thought. How could she have been such a featherwit as to let this come to pass? Only because of a fickle butler whose amorous conquests—lady and maid alike—were too many to count.

"Swinton, do get up," she said sternly, but he only fused his lips to her hand.

"My dearest *darling,* how can I express my feelings to the fullest. I'm overcome with emotion at this—the happiest, the most exalted, moment." His voice rose an octave. "Will you become my wife? Say that you will."

Marianne shuddered and closed her eyes in dismay. "I . . . I'm very honored, of course, but you must let me—"

"Say no more, dearest Marianne. I can see in your maidenly blushes that I have discomfited you. However, I have your father's permission to ask for your hand in marriage, and he led me to believe that you wouldn't be averse to my proposal. He sanctions the union and has promised to endow you with a generous dowry."

"I wish you wouldn't mention dowries at this moment," she mumbled. She tore her hand away. "You must give me some time to think about this."

His face fell. "I had hoped to return to Mother tonight and divulge the happy news. She's looking forward to pressing you to her bosom as her dear daughter-in-law."

"Very kind of her, I'm sure," said Marianne, watching as Swinton heaved himself upright, another seam quaking. "But I can't give you an answer tonight."

He folded his hands behind his back, and the habitually haughty expression he wore returned.

"A great honor; however, Swinton—"

"Yes, it is an honor, Marianne," he said with some sharpness, his adoration vanishing like a puff of smoke. "I wish to have your answer within a sennight, and not a day later. It's not as if you have four or five proposals to choose from."

Anger flared in Marianne's chest at his sudden cool demand, but she said nothing, only turning her gaze demurely to the floor. "I'm sorry, Swinton." Marianne hated herself for getting into this situation. "Then I think I must decline—"

"Marianne!" he exclaimed in shocked tones. "Don't speak so rashly. You shall have your week to ponder my proposal, and I will approach you then, expecting that you've gotten over your obvious confusion. I must have taxed your tender sensibilities to the breaking point."

Marianne stifled another nervous chuckle, fully realizing that Swinton meant to have an affirmative answer one way or another, and that within the next week! If she married him, she would be reduced to an unpaid maid who would have to fulfill his every whim—and his mother's. If Swinton couldn't brag about an abundance of charm, he certainly had a well-developed talent for getting his way.

"I hope to escort you shopping tomorrow, and I shall be at your doorstep on the dot of eleven. Don't be late, Marianne."

"Yes, master," she wanted to shout, and give him a military salute, but ladies did not behave in such an ill-bred fashion. "Thank you, Swinton," she said instead, and escorted him to the front door.

When he'd left, Marianne went in search of her aunt, who was at her embroidery frame by the window in the drawing room. "He offered for me, Aunt Annie," she said.

"I knew that," said Miss Dew, and pursed her mouth in disapproval. "Did you accept him? You said to me once you never would."

"I didn't, but he won't accept a refusal. He's expecting an agreement by today next week."

Miss Dew clapped a hand to her heart. "Dear me. Why, Marianne, why did you invite him to dinner?" She set down her embroidery on the table next to a heap of multicolored skeins of yarn. "You're not the slightest enamored with him."

Marianne sank down on the sofa next to her aunt and studied blindly the white-painted plaster garland above the fireplace. "I'm the greatest fool alive," she said with a profound sigh.

Miss Dew scrutinized her face, and Marianne averted her eyes. "Something has happened to you, Marianne, and I want to know what made you act so rashly as to give Swinton Langley a hint that you're willing to marry him."

"Nothing . . . nothing at all. If I want a family, I must marry a suitor, and I have only one."

"Nonsense! You will find others." Miss Dew's voice took on a prying quality. "*Is* there another gentleman involved?"

"Fiddlesticks, Auntie. As you well know, I have no other gentlemen admirers." Her voice was laced with guilt as the lie came over her lips.

"I saw that you had a lengthy conversation with Mr.

Sherry after the funeral. I don't know when you found the time to nurture his friendship.''

Marianne's eyes widened in horror. "Nurture his *friendship*. Really, Aunt Annie, that's the outside of enough.''

"He's a personable young man," her aunt went on inexorably. "But he won't do, won't do at all.'' She sighed and pulled her embroidery frame back onto her lap. "Marianne, I expect you to have better sense than falling in love with a young man whom you can never marry. Besides, I've heard that he's a terrible flirt, has turned all the maids' heads up at the Folly.''

Marianne's mood darkened. "It doesn't surprise me in the slightest.''

The next morning dawned with a brisk wind and occasional rain showers. With a heavy heart, Marianne donned a walking costume of light gray velvet trimmed with navy braiding and silver buttons. Navy gloves and a navy straw poke bonnet completed the outfit, and she carried her umbrella in one hand and her reticule in the other when Swinton Langley came to fetch her in his outmoded coach. Thank God it was an enclosed vehicle, since gusts of wind did what they could to pull loose satin ribbons, fling off hats, and turn umbrellas inside out.

"Not the best day for an outing," Marianne murmured as Swinton handed her into the carriage. When he sat much too close to her on the seat and started to relate the story of his mother's latest illness, Marianne settled in for a trying morning. She had no one to blame but herself.

Leith tried to calm his fiancée outside the millinery shop in the nearby town of Ashford. "Vivian, I've told you for the tenth time that I had to help Grandmother in this matter.''

Miss Vivian Worton, wearing a charcoal gown with matching pelisse—proper to her state of mourning—and an exquisite black silk bonnet that the wind was trying hard to dislodge, said, ''But dressing up as a butler and snooping in the guests' bedchambers for the letters, why, that goes beyond common decency. It's more than I can stomach, Leith. I'm incredibly disappointed in you. I'm ashamed.'' She turned as if to flee from him, but the wind pushed her back under the awning. She pressed a handkerchief to her eyes. Aunt Fulvia, listening to the conversation, bore a shocked expression that no explanation of his would banish. She held her umbrella raised like a weapon—just in case it needed to fall upon some unfortunate male head, like his.

''*Mr.* Sheridan, I cannot condone this kind of conduct on your part. How will Vivian manage to hold up her head in society if the world discovers what you're doing?'' Her gaze raked over his simple black coat, his mustache, and his spectacles.

Leith raised his hands, palms upward, in a gesture of pleading and said to Vivian, ''We have discussed this endlessly during the last week, and I can't think of another explanation that could better describe the importance of my mission—if you don't understand it now. I'm trying to save us all from scandal.''

Miss Vivian only sobbed into her handkerchief. Aunt Fulvia answered in her place.

''*Really,* Mr. Sheridan, my head has been spinning for a week with the cock-and-bull story you told us, and only the fact that Lady Randome needs us has prevented us from leaving the area. The Dowager Lady Longford would never have written clandestine missives to an admirer. Most likely they bear the print of your own handwriting.''

Leith gave up, realizing he would never gain any ground with Fulvia Worton. The trim old lady gripped Vivian's arm, and they stalked off in the rain, leaving him behind to feel the miserable drip of water from the edge of the awning running down his neck. As he started walking in the opposite direction in search of the nearest tavern, he recalled the letter he'd received from his grandmother only this morning. *Leith, dearest boy,* it started. *You must renew your efforts at finding the love letters and destroy them. The scoundrel has written to me again, this time demanding eight thousand pounds.*

Leith shook his head in consternation. If the blackmailer wasn't Mordecay Follett, who was it? Who was desperate enough for money to keep sending threatening letters to Grandmother? During the last week, he'd searched three of the guest bedrooms: Follett's, Mrs. Fitzwilliam's, and Mrs. Caldway's. He'd found nothing.

Dashing a finger along the dripping rim of his hat, he went inside a smoky tavern called the Hound and Goose and ordered a mug of foaming ale. Sitting at one of the tables with his legs stretched out in front of him, he sipped the brew.

He remembered pressing an ear to the door of the library when the will had been read after the funeral. The old earl's fortune consisted mainly of the entailed estate, which went to his son. That left an adequate jointure to his wife and a few token pounds to the rest of the family to share equally. Exclamations of disappointment had bounced around the library walls at the end of the reading.

The simple fact remained. The title and the fortune belonged to Mordecay Follett upon Nigel's demise.

Who, then, needed money badly enough to put pressure on his grandmother? He'd gleaned from the other servants that Mrs. Fitzwilliam and Mrs. Caldway had more than enough funds left by their deceased husbands. The only one who seemed to have pockets to let was Virgil Fitzwilliam. But surely wouldn't Mordecay sponsor his old friend and relative now that he'd come into wealth? Only time would tell. Time Leith didn't have. Sooner or later someone would recognize him and raise hue and cry. . . .

With a sigh, he emptied the ale mug and went back outside. He would try to find out how desperate Virgil Fitzwilliam really was.

At the street corner he came upon Lottie, one of the maids at the Folly. The prettiest one, he might add, but he wasn't in the mood to chatter with her.

"Why, Mr. Sherry," she cried out in pleasure. "Fancy meetin' you 'ere." She wound her arm around his, and so as not to be rude, he couldn't jerk it away.

"Lottie," he said in a strained voice, "I didn't expect to see you in Ashford."

"'Tis me day off." She dragged him under the awning of the millinery shop and gave him a smile fashioned to dazzle. "Would ye be so kind as to 'elp me choose some new ribbons? Me mother made me an ever so pretty pink dress, and now I need trimmin's."

Before he could protest, she'd pulled him into the milliner's. The clerks gave him covert glances, as he'd only moments before been the object of a young lady's heated argument in front of their shop. "Another young lady?" their eyes seemed to say. Nimble tactics that . . .

"Lottie, why don't we go and have a cup of tea at the local inn," he began, but she was already exclaiming over a sheaf of rainbow-hued ribbons in a box. "Looka 'ere, wouldn't it be ever so lovely with me gown?'' she said, holding up a purple ribbon for his inspection.

"Very appropriate, I daresay," he muttered under his breath. "Now, Lottie, I must—"

"Or this one?" Lottie gave him another bright smile and held a red ribbon up to his face. She giggled. "Ye could use a bright ribbon to 'old up that fierce mustache of yours, Mr. Sherry."

Just at that moment the wind threw the door against the wall, and two sodden females, followed by a sodden gentleman, made their way into the shop. When umbrellas had been furled, exclamations about the weather made, and faces raised, Leith came eye to eye with Marianne Darby. His heartbeat slammed against his ribs as he stared in wonder at her. She stared stormy-eyed at the bright ribbon dangling so closely to his mustache.

"I say," he murmured. "Good morning, Miss Darby, Miss Dew." He viewed their gentleman companion, and didn't like what he saw. He didn't know the identity of their nondescript escort and failed to greet him.

Miss Darby swept by him with her chin held high. "Good morning, Sherry." Her tone of voice could have frozen her saliva into ice, he noted, much dismayed.

She wasn't going to introduce her escort, but why should she? I'm nothing but a lowly butler, after all, Leith thought. The proprietary way the coxcomb was holding Miss Darby's elbow made Leith want to punch his face.

He watched as Marianne stopped by a display of gloves at another counter, at the far side of the shop. She evidently didn't want to come near him. Miss Dew gave him a long, frigid stare and joined Marianne. The young gentleman strutted back and forth on the floor, his hands folded behind him. He puffed out his cheeks in a silent tune.

"Lottie," Leith said under his breath, "who is that gentleman with Miss Darby?"

Lottie threw a cursory glance across the shop. "Why, that's Mr. Langley." She giggled behind her hand. I know 'e's a shockin' gossip, worse than 'is mama, who used to know everyone's business in Spiggott Hollow."

He raised his eyebrows. "Is she deceased?"

"No, Mr. Sherry, but she 'as a new ailment every day. Barely ever leaves 'er bedchamber. They live in that old saggin' mansion right south o' Spiggott Hollow. 'E's set on marryin' Miss Darby. Th' servants at Darby 'Ouse told me." She lowered her voice even more. "''As an eye on 'er dowry, I'm sure. 'E's poor as a church mouse, and Miss Darby's father is quite plump in th' pocket."

"I see," Leith said as jealousy corroded his heart. "Has she accepted his proposal?"

"Mr. Sherry!" Lottie admonished with a saucy smile. "*I* don't work at Darby 'Ouse, so I can't know ever' sordid detail, now, can I?"

"I thought gossip traveled faster than the wind in these parts," Leith said dryly.

"I 'aven't 'eard the sound o' any weddin' bells, 'ave you, Mr. Sherry?"

"No . . . and I don't think we'll hear them anytime soon." Leith pressed his lips together in determination. "I shall find out the truth, Lottie." Before sidling up to Marianne, he waited until Miss Dew was engrossed in a new hat and Swinton Langley was studying the rainy day outside the window.

"Miss Darby, may I have a word?" he asked, watching her stiffening back.

"Certainly not!" she said, and glanced toward Miss Dew.

He was afraid that she would move away from him, but she didn't. Buoyed by that small fact, he continued, "I've heard that congratulations are in order."

She jerked around, facing him in anger. The gloves in her hand fell to the floor, but he ignored them as he was more eager to look into her lovely blue-green eyes than to bend down. She hadn't noticed that she had dropped them.

"Mr. Sherry, I have no idea what you're talking about."

"Don't you?" He inclined his head sideways to indicate Swinton Langley. "I hear you're about to wed that popinjay."

"*Really?*" she said frostily. Two red spots glowed in her cheeks, and her eyes had darkened to a stormy gray. "I thought that you, a distinguished butler, would not stoop to servant-hall gossip."

Leith gave her a smile that didn't sit too comfortably on his face. He yearned to pull her into his arms, not stand inactive like a veritable mutton-brain, discussing her nuptials to another gentleman. "Well, this time I couldn't help but overhear the gossip. It matters greatly to me what you do."

"Mr. Sherry, what I do is my business, and my marital plans are certainly not for the ears of the servants."

"I take it, then, that congratulations are in order," he muttered. "Not that I have the least desire to offer any. Why, the man is an 'old maid,' not a gentleman."

A furious storm seemed to shake her from within and she grabbed the first object she could find, her umbrella, and stabbed the floor with it. Then she stabbed his toe. Biting back a protest, he took a step back. "Miss

Darby,'' he remonstrated gently. ''Control your temper.''

''Don't Miss Darby me. You show unspeakable effrontery by stepping up to me and offering your congratulations when not even the servants at Darby House know what my answer to Mr. Langley was. You're supposed to know your place.''

Leith smiled as hope surged in his heart. ''Then you're not going to marry him. I'm incredibly relieved.''

''I did not say that,'' she said in a low, urgent voice, and aimed for his toes again. ''I didn't explain anything, and if you think you can wring my secrets from me, think again, Sherry. You're the most unpleasant butler I've ever encountered, and the nosiest. Not to mention the falsest, and an incorrigible flirt to boot. It's beyond me to understand how Lady Randome could hire someone like you to replace old Boggs.'' She took a deep breath, before exploding further. In a subdued voice, she continued, ''You're a Lothario, and I mean to tell Lady Randome that you probably were kicked out of your old employment for flirting with the daughters of the house.''

''How severe you are, Miss Darby. Do you care about my past conquests?'' He was starting to enjoy their argument. Clearly her jealousy was speaking. If she was jealous, it meant she cared for him.

''You probably falsified your records and wrote your own recommendation letter. Wait until I inform Lady Randome—''

She was right on that score, Leith thought ruefully. ''You promised not to inform Lady Randome. I have done nothing to earn such an acid threat, Miss Darby.''

''You deserve every vile thing I can think of.''

Leith glanced around the shop, noticing that Miss Dew was conversing with the shopkeeper, and Mr. Langley had stepped outside to greet a crony under the awning. "You're too harsh, Miss Darby, when all I want to do is to kiss you."

She paled, and he thought she would come toward him with her umbrella raised to strike. "I must mean something to you if you feel so strongly about my presence here," he drawled.

That deflated her, and her face drooped as if she were too tired to argue. "If you speak another word to me, I shall complain to the shopkeeper. I shall create a commotion, and you will surely lose your position at the Folly." Her lips quirked wryly, but her eyes still blazed. "Butler attacks lady of sensibility. How does that sound? Not that I'm expecting an answer from you."

"Miss Darby—"

"No! You've sorely tried my patience, and I've had enough for one day."

She glanced past him at Lottie, who was covertly watching them while rummaging in the ribbon box. Hopefully she hadn't heard their conversation, Leith thought.

"Go, Mr. Sherry. Your lady companion seems disappointed that you left her to fend for herself. Another rude move. I ought to warn her about your fickleness."

He took two steps toward her. "Miss Darby, don't marry him," he whispered. "Please don't. *I* love you, and we belong together. Let me prove it. You'll be unhappy with that spinster in pantaloons."

Her eyes widened in shock, and Leith hurried across the room, knowing that she was capable of carrying out her threat of creating a disturbance. If only he could reveal his true identity. Frustration filled him, and he had to storm out of the shop after saying good-bye to a disappointed Lottie.

* * *

I love you, he'd said. Those three words danced, hopped, cavorted, ran, somersaulted through Marianne's head until she thought she would scream out loud with the strain. She took a series of deep breaths, watching Lottie, whom she'd recognized the moment she stepped into the shop. Did anyone notice her confusion?

The fact that the Randome butler loved her was a matter for great hilarity, but the fact that she returned his love was a matter of great doom. How and when had she fallen for that glib scoundrel? Why did her heart cry out every time she saw him?

She noticed vaguely that Lottie had joined her at the glove display. "Good mornin', Miss Darby," she greeted with a small curtsy. "Ye look a trifle peaked. Shall I fetch a chair?"

"No . . . that's not necessary, Lottie." She bent a thoughtful eye on the pretty maid. "Mr. Sherry abandoned you."

Lottie shook her head. "No, 'e wusn't with me. I ran into 'im right outside the ale'ouse." She lowered her voice. "If you must know, 'e was speakin' wi' Miss Worton and 'er aunt earlier. I saw 'em. A mighty row that wus—not that I 'eard what it was all about. Miss Worton flounced off in the rain without botherin' to put up 'er umbrella. Addle-witted foreigner, I'll lay." She lowered her voice even more. "Per'aps they're *lovers.* Wouldn't surprise me, since all the maids at th' Folly are mad about 'im."

Marianne knew that people born and bred in Spiggott Hollow and vicinity scornfully viewed anyone from farther away as a foreigner. She didn't like Lottie's last statement. Of course everyone was mad about him, including herself.

"Miss Darby, are ye sure ye're feelin' quite the thing. Ye're pale, like ye've seen a ghost."

"No, Lottie, I'm fine," Marianne said with more asperity than she intended. "But thank you for your concern." She forced a smile to her lips. "Now I must fetch Miss Dew before she purchases all the hats in the shop." Her knees jellylike, she urged her aunt outside just as soon as their purchases had been concluded.

Swinton Langley held the door for them. "It has stopped raining," he said. He fixed Marianne with a hard stare. "I say, I saw you speaking for a long time with a fellow inside. Someone I know?"

Marianne shook her head.

"That was the Randome butler," Miss Dew said sharply. "What did he have to say to you?"

"It appears that the news of my nuptials has traveled in the village before I've made my decision." She gave Swinton a stern look. "Did you spread the rumors?"

He gave a guilty chuckle. "Ah, well—isn't it a foregone conclusion that you have accepted me?"

For the second time that day, Marianne stabbed her umbrella down in protest. "I have done no such thing, Swinton. I don't want you to spread falsehoods in the village."

He held up his arms as if to ward off her attack. "Such vehemence. I hope you won't show that type of temper once we're married. Mother won't be able to stand any speech louder than a whisper."

Marianne thought her head would explode with wrath. "Is your mother aware of the fact that you've proposed to me?"

Swinton scratched his chin repeatedly. "As a matter of fact, no. I would like it to be a surprise. We'll present her with the engagement as a fait accompli."

"I think we ought to pay her a visit this afternoon."

Swinton flung out his arms in alarm. "Oh, no! She's sedated after a particularly uncomfortable night. We mustn't excite her."

Marianne stepped into the waiting carriage, and as she did so she saw the broad back of Mr. Sherry as he hurried down the street. A sweet surge of longing went through her, and she hated herself for it. She could never marry a butler, and God only knew how many ladies he'd proposed to during his career. Dash it all, but she had fallen for him, just like the maids at the Folly, and Miss Worton, and who knows how many more. If the squire got wind of her infatuation, he'd arrange for a special license to get her shackled to Swinton tomorrow. She would have to convince Swinton that his mother was the only woman in his life, and always would be.

Chapter Nine

JULIA WELLESLY ARRIVED VERY EARLY THE NEXT morning to share breakfast with Marianne and discuss the bazaar that would happen later in the day. It was Saturday, market day. All the farmers from the neighboring villages would drive into Spiggott Hollow, the market cross, stop at the Golden Apple for a mug of ale, and then pause at the bazaar to purchase a ribbon or a comb for their wives and daughters. Julia and Marianne were in charge of the pie-and-cake stall.

Marianne had not slept at all, her head still buzzing with the declaration of love Sherry had uttered at the milliner's shop. How could she be so foolish as to fall in love with a butler—a Lothario of the worst order? she thought as she rubbed her temples where a headache was blossoming.

After washing herself, she put up her hair in a less severe do than usual, curls at the crown and some tendrils spiraling down her neck. She dressed in a light green high-waisted muslin gown with darker bows adorning the front of the bodice, then joined Julia in the breakfast parlor. Her friend wore a severe gown of charcoal sarsenet, a spencer in an even darker hue, and an excited expression on her face.

"I so look forward to the bazaar, Marianne. We'll sell many pies, and make a good contribution toward the church roof. And we'll meet a lot of people."

"We'll make a profit, but perhaps not as great as Lottie and the other maids will make, selling their kisses."

Julia's dark eyes sparkled. "How true, but at least we don't have to buss ale-smelling farmers."

While Marianne was shopping in Ashford, the women of Spiggott Hollow had been busy in the Darby House kitchen baking the pies and cakes. "The question is how to transport the pies to the churchyard."

"Not to worry. I spoke with Sherry this morning, and he said he would deliver the pastry for us."

Marianne's heart jumped into her throat, then sank to her stomach. "That means he's coming here. No need for that, surely? I've a mind to ask Cosmo and Echo Latch. After all, they will come down to set up the tables."

Julia gave an incredulous chuckle. "Cosmo and Echo? I know what will happen. They'll trip over their own feet." She swept out her arm dramatically. "They'll fall with their faces into the pies and ruin every one of them."

Marianne laughed. "That will make them happy. Cosmo enjoys pies of all kinds, especially blueberry." She took a deep breath. "No, we don't need Sherry's help."

Julia gave her a probing stare. "What's the matter, Marianne? You seem to hold the butler in aversion."

"I hear that he is a libertine of the first order."

Julia gave a crow of laughter. "So would I be if I had his face and build. The man's a charmer. The maids are trying to trap him at every corner, but I believe he spends most of his evenings brooding in his pantry, or going about his business. He's immune to their flirting, which is quite odd."

"Perhaps he's a secret tippler." Marianne told herself she ought to stop talking about him, yet she couldn't.

"You mean he tipples Mordecay's brandy at night?" Julia tapped her fingertips thoughtfully on the table. "Hmm, the man wouldn't be human if he didn't have a vice."

Willow, the butler, entered with a silver coffeepot and proceeded to fill their cups. Marianne buttered a slice of toast, and heaped it with strawberry jam.

"Julia, how do you get along with Miss Worton? She seems to be a decisive young lady."

Julia started in on her plate of scrambled eggs. "She's that and more. It seems that Mordecay has taken a great liking to the lady—and she to him. They are forever with their heads together—under the strict chaperonage of Lady Fulvia, of course."

Hope quivered in Marianne's chest. Perhaps she'd imagined a liaison between Sherry and the lovely Miss Worton. Perhaps there was no sordid affair of the heart. *Perhaps he truly loves me. I'm foolish, dreaming about something that can never be.* She chewed and swallowed, wishing she could wipe Lester Sherry and his smiling eyes from her mind.

"Well, Sherry will be here in twenty minutes," Julia said, glancing at the watch pinned to her dress.

"Very well, since you arranged this, you can wait for him here. I'll go down to the church and supervise Cosmo and Echo."

Julia's gaze filled with suspicion, probing Marianne's deepest secrets. "I'd say you're hiding something from me."

"Fustian." Marianne's face grew hot, and she cursed the day she had laid eyes on the impudent Randome butler. "Nothing, Julia, nothing worth mentioning, anyway."

She fled out of the house just in time to see Sherry disappear inside through the kitchen entrance. Thank God she'd escaped him.

The setting up of the tables in front of the church went without any problems. Cosmo and Echo didn't trip over their feet, and the maids from Randome's Folly did not giggle unduly as Sherry brought in the pies on a push wagon. Marianne blushed and glanced to the ground as he arrived. She busied herself separating the doilies that would be placed under the pies and cakes.

He admired the painted sign above the stall, reading it aloud: "Delicious Cakes and Pies." He turned to her, his voice persuasive. "Miss Darby," he began, and she felt his full attention descending on her. She kept her eyes averted.

"Didn't I warn you yesterday, Mr. Sherry? Don't you dare speak to me," she said heatedly. She glanced up, right into his intensely blue eyes, and something inside her heart, a brick fortification, a granite stockade perhaps, crumbled. Speechless, she stared into the depths of him, seeing only love and admiration.

"Go away, Sherry," she said breathlessly. From the corner of her eye she noticed Cosmo coming up to the stall, and behind him Julia. "We can manage from now on—*without* you."

"Very well," he said with a hitch of disappointment in his voice. "But remember what I said yesterday in Ashford. It's all true, every word of it."

"I'm sure you rehearsed your little speech for quite some time, to get it perfect, and tilted your tone of voice in just the right inflection." She tore her gaze away from him. "Good-bye."

To her relief, he didn't argue. An inexplicable loss filled her heart at his departure.

The day wore on, the churchyard filling with hundreds of people from all the villages around Spiggott Hollow. Laughter and chatter rose toward the sky. Awnings flapped in the breeze, and some curious sea gulls circled and screeched overhead. Marianne and Julia sold all their pies in an hour, and there were only five cakes left when the hot afternoon drew to an end.

To stretch her legs, Marianne went around to the other stalls, admiring ribbons and bows in one stall, and sewing implements in another, where she bought a dozen tortoiseshell buttons. Some stalls held fruits, exotic oranges, limes, and bananas, others held old books donated from the stately homes in the area.

An urchin with strawberry-pie filling around his mouth came up to her and pressed a folded note into her hand. "For ye, Miss Darby." He dashed off before she could ask who the sender was.

Frowning in consternation, she opened the missive and read:

> *Marianne, your eyes have stolen my soul,*
> *Your smile, my breath.*
> *I read what is writ upon my heart,*
> *Your name, your smile, your love, and*
> *My love, for you.*

Marianne jerked her head up, glancing among the burly farmers for Sherry's tall form, but he was nowhere to be seen. She knew he had written the love poem, but why give it to her now?

Suddenly she came eye to eye with a leering Swinton Langley. He took her hand. "Miss Darby, I've missed you terribly. Life without you is an empty, barren road." He peered at the note in her hand and read the poem. "Since you seem enamored of romantic verse, I sat all night composing one for you."

Stunned by his sudden appearance and amorous talk, she could not respond at first. Confused, she held out her note. "Did . . . did *you* write this, Swinton?"

He glanced uncertainly at her, and she thought he took an inordinate amount of time to answer. "Why . . . yes, of course I wrote this. Did you like it?"

Marianne scrutinized his narrow face. She could have sworn that Sherry had written the poem. It held deep feeling, and she could hardly believe that Swinton harbored any tender emotions for her. "Why, that was a lovely poem, Swinton." She fought to subdue an urge to run away and hide. She needed to sort out her feelings and calm her nerves. Alone.

The booming laughter, the loud discussions of the farmers around her made her head reel. People bumped into her from all sides.

"I felt that now—since we're on the threshold of marriage—you wouldn't take amiss a few lines of written adoration."

"Swinton—I must return to my post at the cake stall." She tore away from him and rushed blindly through the crush of people to the back of the church, right close to the shed where Sherry had kissed her for the first time. That kiss had changed her life.

She sat on the church steps of the side entrance. A huge elm cast its shadow over the facade, and she was grateful for the seclusion. Tears started rolling down her face, and she dabbed at them furtively. Her friends and family would laugh if they knew she was crying because of a butler who collected "conquests." She'd better go home before someone found her here. She'd tell Julia that a sudden headache had overwhelmed her.

Just as she passed the wide trunk of the elm, she was startled from her reverie by a deep male voice. "Good afternoon, Miss Darby." She knew that voice, and that warm smile under a bristling mustache.

"Are you spying on me, Sherry?" Anger replaced her sorrow, yet she could not shout, or move away. She dashed the back of her hand across her face to wipe any trace of her tears away.

"Yes, as a matter of fact, I am."

She had a heated retort on her lips, but he stalled her. "Don't fly into a pet. I saw you run toward the back, and I got worried." His gaze burned into her, and she found she couldn't breathe.

"What has upset you, Miss Darby?"

She lowered her eyes and twisted her handkerchief around her fingers. "Oh, many things, many *stupid* things."

"Am I guilty of provoking those tears?" He stepped forward, and she noticed that he'd loosened his neckcloth and opened the top of his shirt. It was hot, but suddenly she felt hotter inside than out as she viewed dark tufts of hair in the shirt opening. A very improper sight, she thought in a haze of confusing emotions.

He held out his hand. "Come here, Miss Darby . . . Marianne."

She didn't move, and his voice turned more insistent. "Come to me."

Too weak to refuse, she placed her hand in his firm

grip, and he pulled her behind the tree trunk, away from prying eyes. He pressed her close, and she was highly aware of the steely well-defined muscles of his chest. Her gaze locked with his beautiful blue eyes, cool, clear pools that seemed to heat up and start blazing the longer she looked at him.

"I take it you're looking for a bit of dalliance," she said in a dreamy, faraway voice.

"More than that, much more," he whispered, stroking her hairline with one fingertip. His lips quirked upward. "Not that there's anything wrong with dalliance. Passes the time quite agreeably."

She pushed against his chest to get away from his arms encircling her waist. "You're incorrigible."

He held her tighter. "You should learn to relax, my darling," he said. "Learn to accept a joke for what it is." His face bent toward hers, and she was only aware of his virile scent, the intoxicating light in his eyes, the sooty eyelashes and the hard cheekbones . . . the soft ear-lobes under her fingers . . . lips, hard yet tender, warmly demanding on hers. With a moan, she closed her eyes, savoring the pressure of his mouth, the silky tongue that mated with her own, provoking a euphoria she had never known. Sounds receded, summer scents became part of their kiss, fruit, blossom, a fulfillment that tinted everything with poignancy. Marianne wondered if he shared her deep intoxication. . . .

Leith realized how he'd—up until this moment—lived a deprived life, now that he was holding the woman of his heart in his arms. He didn't want to let go of her, not now, not ever. Softness, curves, tickling curls that smelled of honeysuckle and summer sun, peachy cheeks, suspicious yet dreamy eyes. Goddess painted in pastels with her quirky gait that so ashamed her, but endeared her to him.

He slowly lifted his head, gazing into her melting eyes. "Say that you love me, Marianne."

"Oh . . . don't start your nonsense, Sherry—"

He pressed her closer, round breasts so intimate against his chest, only separated from his skin by starched linen and thin muslin. "Say the words. I need to hear them."

Her bottom lip trembled alarmingly, but he only smiled at her. "Well? Didn't this kiss convince you?"

"I love you," she whispered, her eyes widening in horror. Her voice rose, tinged with panic. "I'm in love with a butler. Papa will never accept you."

"Don't worry about anything. I'll take care of Squire Darby."

"He's the most stubborn person to walk on this earth."

He nuzzled her downy cheek and cupped the back of her head as tenderly as if she were a newborn babe. "No, Marianne, my grandmother is the most stubborn person on earth."

That elicited a chuckle from her. Tears glistened in her eyes, but she continued laughing, and he'd never felt happier. She had finally admitted her feelings to a—butler. It was time to confess his true identity, and as soon as the matter of the love letters was cleared up, he would approach Squire Darby—the second most stubborn person in the world.

"Marianne, I need to explain—" he began, but she stood on her toes, pulling down his head with both hands. He had no choice but to kiss her dewy, intoxicating mouth again, and again.

So lost was he that he first thought he was hearing

voices in his head. He slowly lifted his eyes, relaxing his
embrace as he noticed Marianne stiffening. Right behind
her stood the gentleman who had escorted her to Ashford
on the previous day. Hellfire and thunder glowed in his
eyes, and his pale face had a green tinge.

"Miss Darby!" the fellow cried out in outraged tones.
"*What* are you doing?"

Leith dropped his arms with an apologetic smile at
Marianne. She would be ruined unless he offered for her
on the spot—but like she'd said, Squire Darby was
unlikely to accept a butler. Nor would he be eager to
accept the Honorable Leith Sheridan, who had deceived
an entire village with his butler disguise. He had to
protect Marianne from shame at all costs. Marianne tore
away from him and clasped her hand over her mouth.
Her eyes widened, darkened in confusion.

"Swinton," she said lamely, fearing her swain's
retribution.

"*What* is this fellow doing here?" Swinton demanded
frostily. "And *what* are you doing in his arms? Answer
me this instant."

"Swinton, let me explain—" she began apologeti-
cally, but could not find words to excuse her sharing of
heated kisses with the Randome butler behind a tree. A
sinking feeling went through her.

"I don't want any lies from you," Swinton said
contemptuously. "I want an explanation from him. I
know who he is—a *butler*. A chaser of women." He
poked his index finger into Sherry's chest, and Sherry
slapped away his hand. Marianne worried that the butler
would lose his temper. One thing was certain, Sherry
would have to look for another position after this.
Swinton would spread this news around the village faster
than lightning—wouldn't he? Perhaps not, if he was

afraid of ridicule. She cast about for a quick solution to the problem.

"You have the advantage of me. . . ." said Sherry. He quirked an eyebrow at Marianne, as cool as a cucumber, as if this current situation wasn't extremely ticklish.

"Mr. Swinton Langley, Mr. Sherry," Marianne introduced feebly.

"Then Mr. Langley, I think you saw what was going on. Kissing. You do know about the act of kissing?"

Swinton opened and closed his mouth repeatedly. Fury mottled his sallow cheeks. "Of all the impudence! I want to see you on your knees for this, Sherry."

"I'm not a beggar," Sherry drawled, and leaned back against the tree, crossing his arms over his chest.

"You . . . you were *kissing* my *fiancée*," Swinton babbled.

"Do you want to call me out?" Sherry asked icily.

Marianne gasped. This was going badly. She pulled Swinton's arm repeatedly as that young man looked as if he would explode at any moment. "Swinton, listen to me," she said sternly.

He pulled away, but she gripped his arm again. "If you as much as whisper about this in the village, you can never marry me. You'll ruin the reputation of your own fiancée," she said.

He looked at her, confusion filming his eyes.

"You do want to marry me, don't you?" she went on, hearing Sherry gasping with wrath beside her.

Swinton nodded vigorously. "You've decided, then? You agree to marry me . . . ?"

"Yes, but you must keep quiet, now and forever, otherwise I'll not marry you." She dropped her hand, studying his face as calculation sneaked across his features. No Marianne—no dowry, she could read in his eyes.

She shot a quick glance at Sherry, noticing the storm growing in his eyes. He looked quite pale. "I will marry you, Swinton, if you don't breathe a word of this."

"Marianne!" Sherry exclaimed, his jaw set in anger. "You fickle . . . lying—"

"I'm only trying to save your employment—yet again," Marianne said haughtily. "You should be grateful."

"I don't care a fig for my position," he said between clenched teeth. He leaned over her, and she wished she could curl her arms around him. "You said you lo—"

"Shhh," she said, holding her finger against his lips. "Mr. Langley was so kind as to propose to me a week ago, and I promised him an answer by today."

Sherry paled even further, then mortification flooded his face with red. With one hard look at her, he stalked away. Marianne thought her legs would collapse under her as the ordeal had been overcome. Yet the outcome was quite different than she would have wished.

"Good riddance to bad rubbish!" Swinton spat.

Marianne thought of many unladylike expressions to hurl at her odious fiancé, but a real lady subdued such urges. She was a lady despite the fact that she'd given her heart to a butler.

Chapter Ten

FOR MARIANNE THE BAZAAR WAS OVER, EVEN THOUGH many farmers still roamed among the stalls buying trinkets. After Swinton had left her alone behind the tree, she suffered a bout of tears. She dried her eyes, adjusted her hair, and joined Julia at the cake stall. Perhaps seeing Julia would bring sanity back to her life.

"What happened to you, Marianne? You just disappeared. You look pale and sad."

Marianne wished she could confide in her friend, but Julia could not keep a secret for very long. She might be shocked at Marianne's behavior. Why, she was shocked herself that she had given her heart to a wholly unsuitable gentleman. She was reckless beyond belief, and unreliable. Her father would be disappointed in her if he found out.

Julia continued, "Sherry stalked by the stall, so angry I thought he would strangle anyone who spoke to him. Do you know why he was up in the boughs?"

"Perhaps someone gave him a well-deserved beargarden jaw,'' Marianne said with a wry smile. "He's not a proper gentleman—for a butler, I mean.''

"No . . . I find his profession was a poor choice. He should have been a gambler or a gentlemen's-club owner—''

"—or a professional flirt, or an actor at the King's Theatre,'' Marianne filled in. "Or a court jester.''

Julia looked at her closely. "You sound bitter, and your eyes are red-rimmed.''

Marianne fought back a fresh bout of tears. What a muddle she'd made of her life, but she could not divulge her secret to Julia. She clutched her forehead. "I have a terrible headache. Would you mind if I left? I need to rest in a dark room with a cold cloth over my eyes.''

Julia was full of sympathy. "Yes, you must go home. I'll fetch Miss Dew for you. She's helping at the fruit stand, but she must accompany—''

Marianne shook her head vehemently. "No! I'd rather be alone. Anyway, it's only a two-minute walk home.''

Before Julia could protest, Marianne slunk away from the bazaar. She went along the side of the church wall toward the lych-gate. She passed the climbing rose that showed a profusion of buds at the corner of the gate, and entered the lane.

She heard sounds of horses and creaking wheels. A man walked ahead of her. Gasping, she recognized the broad back of Mr. Sherry, only ten paces farther ahead. A carriage had just pulled up beside him, the four horses snorting. "Ho!'' the coachman shouted.

A man in a tall beaver hat leaned out the coach window and waved at Mr. Sherry, who had flattened himself against the stone wall as if trying to hide.

"I say! Leith Sheridan, old fellow, what in the world are you doing in this godforsaken village wearing that ridiculous mustache," the stranger cried out. "I heard Vivian is in hot pursuit, so I came down to watch. She wrote to me, asking my opinion on this your latest scheme. I say, you're a downy one, Leith. Haha—hah."

"Horry Fishborne. What are *you* doing here, old codger?"

The horses cavorted, tossing their heads. "I'm visiting a crony at Ashford. Right now I'm going up to the Folly, to offer my condolences. I'll speak to you in the *butler's pantry.*" The stranger laughed uproariously. "Wait until the *ton* hears about this!"

Leith took two angry steps toward the coach. "Don't you dare say a word, Horry, or I'll call you out."

"Touchy, aren't you? We'll see." The stranger's coachman let the horses have their heads, and the equipage rattled up the road toward the Folly. Sherry turned his head just as Marianne stalked up to him.

Without a word, she yanked off his mustache, first one side, than the other, and dropped them to the ground.

"Aoow," he cried, and clapped his hand to the tender spot above his upper lip. "Don't do that!"

"Oh, yes, the butler sports a luxurious mustache to cover an embarrassing scar. Yes, indeed, and he's half-blind, so he has to wear glasses." She tore off his spectacles and tossed them into the brambles by the stone wall. Then she tried to pull his hair off, thinking it was a wig, but it didn't budge.

"You've lied to me, Sherry—Leith! You've lied from the moment we met," she cried, hot tears blurring her sight, and choking her throat. "You call Horace Fishborne, the Marquess of Worthington, Horry, and you parade under the silly name of Lester Sherry. *Who* are you?" She took a swing at him, missing. "I . . . I *hate* you!"

He picked up the mustache pieces she'd flung in the dust and pocketed them. Then he gripped her upper arms, holding her steady. "Listen to me, Marianne. I tried to explain earlier, behind that tree, but you interrupted me with some very agreeable kisses."

"You were the one who forced the kisses on me," she said, her voice choking with emotion. That wasn't quite true, of course, but at this point, it didn't matter who had kissed whom. She dried her tears, and made another unsuccessful attempt to punch his jaw.

Leith was loath to let one of Marianne's furious swings hit his face. Anger tightened his chest, and he pulled her, not too tenderly, along the path that led past the vicarage, along a huge stand of lilacs, down a slope to the lazy river below. He set her down on a tussock of grass and sank down beside her. "I shall tell you everything, and you will listen."

"I warn you, I don't want to hear any more lies."

He held up his hands, giving her an exasperated glance. "I promise, no more lies."

He touched her cheek and whispered, "What happened behind that tree was true. I do love you, Marianne."

He took her hands in both his and launched into the story of his grandmother and her missing love letters. "The morning I stepped into Mrs. Fitzwilliam's bedchamber, and you were there, I was looking for the missing letters."

"I remember finding it strange that you would mistake her room for Mordecay's."

"I did suspect Mordecay of extorting money from Grandmother since he was debt-ridden at that time. But he's a wealthy man now, and someone is still threatening

Grandmother. It can't be him; he doesn't need the money.''

Marianne furrowed her brow in thought. "I thought all of the Randomes are well-off."

"They are, or one of them is pretending to be well-off. I now believe that Virgil Fitzwilliam might be the culprit. After what I overheard one night, I'm inclined to believe he has gambling debts." He heaved himself up onto his knees and captured her face between his hands. "Marianne, do you understand why I had to enact this subterfuge? I didn't want to, but I had no choice lest someone recognize me. Besides, I told you that Grandmother is a stubborn woman. There's no gainsaying her when she gets an idea into her head. The butler disguise was her idea."

Marianne pinned him with a probing glare. "And who is your grandmother?"

"Antonia, the Dowager Baroness of Longford."

Marianne gasped. "And you are . . . ?"

In unison they said, "The Honorable Leith Sheridan."

Marianne jumped up, moving away from him as if loath to touch him. He followed. "What's the matter, Marianne? Aren't you relieved that I'm not a butler, after all?"

She shook her head. "I'm not relieved. When I was in London two years ago, you had a reputation for crushing young ladies' hearts. You're a philanderer, and always will be. I can't trust you, and if Father discovers your game, he'll never let you come near me again."

"I didn't *plan* on crushing any hearts, dammit. The debutantes followed me around wherever I went, throwing themselves at me. I had to be very firm lest they scream that I had seduced them. I tell you, I didn't kiss a single one of them like I kissed you—with my heart."

Marianne didn't know what to think. She stared at him with uncertainty, yearning to believe him. He looked sincere, but he could have persuaded any number of young females of his love—as he'd been trying to persuade her with his kisses. He'd been very successful with her, and her knees weakened once again as she remembered their embrace behind the tree. He probably never met failure in matters of the heart.

"You were not a gentleman when you kissed me that first time in the shed," she reminded him. "I interpreted the kiss as the clumsy effort of a butler, who didn't know better. But you were Leith Sheridan then, and you knew what you were doing."

He made a pleading gesture, and her heart softened. "I lose all coherent thought when I'm with you, Marianne. No other woman has had that effect on me. Truly. I know I behaved in an ungentlemanly fashion, but believe me, my emotions overcame me."

She gave him a doubtful glance. "How many times have you said those same words to other besotted ladies?"

His shoulders slumped. "Oh, Marianne, don't torture me. Why do you have to be suspicious of my every action?"

"Really, Leith, you have deceived me successfully all this time. What would stop you from deceiving me again and again?"

"You have to trust me. Once the matter of Grand-mother's love letters is cleared up, I will approach the squire and request your hand in marriage."

"As you well know, I'm already promised to marry Swinton Langley. Father has already made a tentative settlement with him." She glanced away, feeling the pain of her pledge to Swinton Langley just to save Leith's employment. "I promised to marry another man just to protect you, and you're not a butler! You don't even *care* if you lose your position at Randome's Folly."

He stepped up to her and swept her into his arms. "I tried to stop you, but you wouldn't listen. You're going to marry me. You must tell Swinton Langley he has to look for another bride."

Marianne began to protest, but his mouth came down hard on hers. Any bodily contact with him made her lose her thread of thought. She could not deny that his embrace was the most delicious experience. How could she push him away when his touch sent her into bliss? Her legs buckled and he lifted her up. Before she knew what had happened, she was lying stretched out on the grass, his arms around her.

A bumblebee droned by, a warm breeze shivered the leaves of an aspen right above their heads, and downy clouds floated across the sky. "Sherry—Leith, I don't think Father . . . If anyone should find us here—"

His kiss silenced her again, and then there was only his touch, the virile scent of him, the pressure of his hard chest against hers. His hand traveled the length of her body, then up again. Every thought of decency fled from her mind, and she wanted to discover what love meant besides kissing.

Leith sensed her surrender, and he knew he could have made love to her right there on the grass bank, only half a mile away from the bazaar. He longed desperately to follow his impulses, but it would be insane. He had compromised her as it was. With difficulty, he pulled his hand away from her body and lifted his head to gaze down at her sweet innocent face. Her unfocused eyes had darkened with passion, and her lips were half-open, her warm breath fanning his cheek.

"Marianne, I desire you, but I can't take you here, like this. I want to do the honorable thing, put a wedding band on your finger before I make you mine." His voice was hoarse, and he found it almost impossible to tear himself away from her.

She blinked twice to focus, then shook her head in confusion. Blushing, she raised herself up on her elbows, and he eased away from her, but remained close enough to feel the heat of her skin. He picked dry grass from her hair, which was falling down over her shoulders in golden skeins, and smoothed her gown.

"Aren't you going to take what I was ready to give?" she asked huskily, her earnest gaze piercing him.

He shook his head and clenched his jaw to put a rein on his escalating desire. "No, that would be unfair to you."

"I thought you'd be eager to press home any advantage, like your counterpart, Don Juan."

He frowned. "'Tis twaddle, and you know it."

She rolled toward him. "I don't think I'll ever know what love between a man and a woman is, unless—" She bit her lip, blushing. "Certainly not with Swinton Langley. I've wondered—waited for a long time to find out. I never thought a gentleman would want to touch me because of my deformed hip."

She sounded so forlorn, and he read the ache in her eyes. With a groan, he gathered her to him and covered her flushed face with tiny kisses. Desire pounded through him, filling every vein with liquid fire.

"Darling Marianne, I want to touch you, every inch of you," he murmured against her lips. "Even your deformed hip, especially it. I would like to caress away your pain."

"It rarely hurts," she whispered, her eyes sparkling

like stars. "You almost sound like you admire my flaw."

"Those make you human. Otherwise I might think I'm holding a goddess in my arms. That would be daunting, to say the least."

"You're a silver-tongued devil."

He chuckled. "Better silver-tongued than just a devil. I can't abide the thought of you believing that I'm that black of a creature."

She punched him lightly in the shoulder. "You always have a glib answer to everything."

He grew serious. "I haven't told you, but I'm not as flawless as you might think." This announcement got her entire attention. "Yes . . . I went to war and was wounded on the Peninsula. Took a bullet through my lung and lived. A miracle, isn't it?"

She nodded, and her eyes clouded with worry. "Are you in pain now?"

He shook his head. "No, but one of my lungs seems weak, and I lose my breath easily. According to the doctors, I'm cured and will live till I'm ninety."

"Do you feel . . . less worthy because of the wound?"

"No, why should I? Many soldiers received worse wounds than I."

"At least your weakness doesn't show on the outside."

Leith sighed. "It's enough that I feel it. However, what I'm trying to say is that you aren't worth less because of a minor disability—not even if it were a great one. In fact, it makes you special. Without it, you might have turned into a demanding, spoiled lady who has no thought for anyone but herself. Instead you're thoughtful and kind."

Marianne wrinkled her brow. "I've never thought

about it that way, but you have a point." A smile dawned on her face. "I think you're lifting a lifelong burden from my shoulders."

"Your old fear won't leave that easily, but it's a start."

"Oh, Leith . . ."

He kissed her, invading her mouth with his tongue, and she was hopelessly lost in the wonder of his touch. She swam in a haze of happiness as long as the kiss lasted. Every one of his caresses brought her deeper into a love that felt entirely right. She had waited to be loved; she had waited for a man who dared to show his love for her, and she refused to think further than the promise that Leith would make her his, soon. She refused to let her doubts take hold and corrode her mind.

A glow spread through her, a glow so bright she felt entirely illuminated from inside. Happiness lived in that brightness, and Marianne felt in awe of such strong emotion.

Tears welled in her eyes, and she opened them, gazing directly into Leith's clear blue ones.

"Am I holding you too hard?" he asked, his happy face clouding momentarily with worry. He loosened his arms around her.

"No, not at all. That kiss made heaven and earth move."

"It's only the first taste. There's so much more to come," he said with such tenderness that she believed theirs would be a life filled with loving. He raised himself above her on his elbows. "I have adored you, my darling, from the moment I set eyes on you up at the Folly."

Marianne made a noise of disbelief. "You must be lying."

"No . . . something struck my soul when I glanced into your eyes. Truly. Cupid's arrow it's called. I never believed in Cupid, but now I do."

She pushed him lightly in the chest, but he looked so earnest.

"In your eyes, Marianne, I saw a sea, a blue-green sea, and I found that I wanted to drown in it, in you."

Marianne's heartbeat slammed against her ribs. "Your words take my breath away. How can I trust such a smooth-tongued rogue as you?"

He cradled her face between his palms. "Marianne, I want you to trust me."

"Yes . . ." she whispered. "I will trust you. Perhaps." As the glow slowly receded the sounds of the bazaar, and the quacking of some ducks in the water, brought her back to reality. She blushed and stood, brushing off her skirt. "Oh, my, I must have lost my sanity to stay here with you."

"Yes, and so did I." He rolled onto his feet and righted his neckcloth. "We took a terrible risk," he said. "I don't want to compromise you, yet I couldn't stop myself from stealing a precious moment with you alone."

Marianne smoothed her hair and rearranged the curls. She still glowed inside, and this moment she trusted him. But would she when they parted? She hastily pushed that thought away.

"You must go home, Marianne, before anyone notices that you're missing." He fell to his knees and rubbed at a grass stain on the flounce of her gown. Then he made sure the straps of her kid slippers were in place.

"You're very adept at the details of a lady's toilette," she chided gently. "Much practice, I gather?"

He didn't respond, only gave her an exasperated glare.

He stood and made sure that her gown hung straight. "You look good enough to eat, Marianne," he said softly. "However, I must restrain myself." He touched her cheek. "I can't remove that rapturous look on your face, nor can I rub out the fact that your lips have been well kissed today."

She stood on her toes and wound her arms around his neck. "Just one more," she begged, and he dutifully complied.

Dazed, and hands clasped like lovers, they walked up the path. Leith dropped her hand just as they arrived at the vicarage.

Marianne raised her gaze, and right there, waiting at the gate, was Swinton. He gave her a look full of hatred, then hurried down the road toward Darby House.

Marianne's spirit plummeted. "Oh, no, he must have seen us coming up the lane holding hands."

"Or perhaps more," said Leith, his tone of voice predicting that great problems would arise in the near future.

"We shall prevail. I shall speak with Swinton today and tell him I can't marry him." Preoccupied, Marianne glanced at Leith. "I did forget to ask you one question, Leith. Who is Vivian Worton? What does she mean to you?"

Leith took a deep breath, and a shutter fell over his face. "Oh, God, I completely forgot about her." After a thoughtful pause, he said, "Vivian is my fiancée."

Chapter Eleven

"YOUR *FIANCÉE*?" MARIANNE STIFFENED AS ICY FEAR filled her body. "Why didn't you tell me immediately, while you confessed about your charade?"

"I would have told you, but I forgot." Obviously embarrassed, he dashed his hands through his hair. "Truly, I forgot. The last person on my mind was Vivian. It was unforgivable not to explain about her, though."

"Your *fiancée* the last person on your mind?" She stared at him as if she'd discovered some unmentionable foulness. What a fool she'd been to listen to his compliments, designed for seduction. She'd fallen for his every trick since that first kiss in the shed, like a ripe plum falling from the tree. The weight of the truth seemed to crush her insides.

His eyes darkened with worry. "Marianne, don't look at me like that. I'll find a way to break off with Vivian."

"A true gentleman does not break off his engagement. It's for the sole discretion of a lady to jilt a gentleman."

"I know that!" He slammed his palm against his thigh

in frustration. "Good God, Marianne, there must be a way." He moved toward her as if to enfold her in an embrace, but she pushed him away.

"Don't try any new tactics with me. You found it convenient to inform me *after* our heated kisses that you're already betrothed."

"A few hours ago, you didn't know my true identity. I explained about that, but I failed to tell you everything. I was too overcome—"

"Stop talking. I can't bear any more lame excuses." Marianne clapped her hands to her ears and struggled to contain her anger. "At least I would never have suspected that you were affianced to Miss Worton when you were Butler Sherry. Of all the consummate effrontery—"

"Don't get into a pelter, Marianne. Let's discuss this in a calm and logical manner."

Marianne pushed him, so that he staggered back against the brambles lining the stone wall around the church. "What other shocking surprises are you planning to divulge? That you have five illegitimate sons, or that you've made love to *fifty* virgins in your time. Was I to be the fifty-first, mayhap?"

"Calm down, Marianne. I don't make a habit of—"

"Spare me your explanations, please! You have trifled with me, and I won't forget that." Without another word, she turned around and headed toward home. Tears blinded her eyes, and her heart ached so much she thought it was surely going to burst. But the sting of her mortification was the hardest burden to bear. She could never look herself in the mirror again. *Fool!*

When she arrived home, dusk had fallen. The perfume from the flowers in the borders hung in the still air, but Marianne, who often enjoyed a stroll in the garden in the evening, rejected any thought of strolling. She longed for her bedchamber and her pillow, which would muffle her sobs. But she didn't go in at first. She hid in the stables to ease some of her pain among her father's beloved horses. Unfortunately, this time, they could not soften her sorrow, no matter how many whickers and snorts greeted her, or how many velvet muzzles sought her hand.

Finally she had to go inside. Pressing her handkerchief to her face, she crossed the dark hallway and began climbing the stairs. The fifth step creaked, and as she stepped on the sixth her father's voice rang out in the gloom.

"Marianne? Is that you? I want to talk to you. Come to my study."

Marianne froze, panic filling her. She patted her hair distractedly and righted her gown. Would her father notice anything amiss? Would he see that she'd spent part of the afternoon kissing a young gentleman other than Swinton Langley?

On trembling legs, she went to the door of the study. "Papa? Are you sitting in the dark with only one branch of candles lit? Why, I shall ask Willow to fetch—"

"Come here, daughter." The squire sounded tired, and somewhat stern.

Marianne stepped closer to the circle of light on the desk. She barely dared to breathe as apprehension tightened up her throat. "What is the matter?"

"You must explain that to me, Marianne," he said, his voice rising to the condemning tones of a preacher.

"I don't know what you mean, Papa."

He rose ponderously and stepped around the desk to face her. "Swinton Langley came here in a rare taking an hour ago, and claimed that he'd seen you *kissing* the

Randome butler behind a tree, then holding hands with him two hours later outside the vicarage.''

Thank God he hadn't seen more than that, Marianne thought with a small sigh of relief. If he had, Papa would not be this calm. She glanced into her sire's probing eyes, and knew it would be a mistake to lie.

"Yes, Papa. I kissed the butler, and it was an unforgivable blunder on my part." She could tell her father about Leith's real identity, but then he would storm up to the Folly and reveal the impostor. Lady Antonia Longford would be the one to be hurt the most, if Leith could not find the love letters before the truth of his identity came out. Marianne wanted to denounce him, to make him hurt, like she hurt at this moment, but her spite didn't stretch that far. Even now she had to protect him.

"A blunder?" the squire shouted. "You are ruined. It was a demmed feather-witted thing to do. Why?"

Marianne took a step back as her father towered over her. He had a violent temper at times, but he'd never beaten her. "I don't know, Papa."

"Swinton told me that earlier today you promised to marry him."

Marianne nodded miserably. "I did."

The squire stomped back around the desk and flung himself into his chair. "Then so you shall, before your reputation is ruined beyond repair. I shall write to the archbishop for a special license and ask Swinton to carry it to Canterbury on the morrow."

Marianne wrung her hands. "No, Papa! I really don't want to marry Swinton. It would be a terrible mistake."

He put down his quill, very carefully, very precisely. His eyes were dark with fury, condemning. "Then why did you tell him you would? I've never known you to be fickle. I've settled with Langley. You can't change your mind now." He folded his hands over his broad chest. "In fact, I let you take your time deciding. If you'd said no, I would have abided by your decision, Marianne. That's because you've always acted in a reliable, responsible way. Why this change of character?"

Marianne could not tell him the truth, but she couldn't lie either. She settled for an explanation that was partly true. "Swinton was very insistent, and I've always believed that no gentleman in his right mind would care to marry me." She touched her hip. "Because of my infirmity. Swinton was—is—my last resort."

"But you just said you're not going to marry him."

"Oh, Papa, let me speak to him and explain everything before you send him to Canterbury. I don't want to act in haste."

The squire muttered something unintelligible under his breath and rose. "Very well," he said with a sigh. "I know I shouldn't listen to you, but—"

"Thank you, Papa." Like she usually did before going up to bed, she headed toward him for a kiss on the cheek, but something in his eyes stopped her.

"Don't thank me until you've explained why you let that ramshackle butler kiss you."

Marianne stood motionless, as if attached to the floor, staring at his suspicious face.

"I . . . I was foolish," she said haltingly. "That's all."

"He's a handsome fellow, by all means, but I think you would show some more sense than to have your head turned by such a man. He'll destroy you, if you let him." The squire raised his voice once again. "You don't know this, Marianne, but I've seen him moon after you in the village. I'm very observant when it comes to my own daughter, and I know that the fellow will take advantage of an innocent female.''

"The maids . . . are in love with him," she whispered, tortured by the thought.

"Well, they should beware lest they find themselves in the family way. Mark my words, once the fat is in the fire, the butler will disappear from this village mysteriously one night. I have a mind to speak up to Lord Randome about this and have the fellow dismissed.''

"No! It was as much my fault as his. I don't want to have his dismissal on my conscience. Papa, I promise to be careful,'' Marianne added between stiff lips. "I shall behave properly in the future. You shall have no reason to be ashamed of me.''

"Very good.'' The squire chuckled suddenly as if a burden had fallen from his shoulders. "I don't blame you for wanting to kiss a handsome scoundrel when faced with the prospect of marrying Swinton Langley. But at least I give the silly fellow Langley credit, he won't have a string of mistresses to embarrass you once you're wed.''

"No,'' said Marianne with a deep sigh, "he'll have his mother.''

"You know, he suggested that I lock you up in your room until the wedding.''

"He has some strange views on trust,'' Marianne said, yet she couldn't blame Swinton. By instinct, he must have sensed what was happening between her and Leith. Swinton would not speak of it, however, since that would forfeit the dowry she would bring to their marriage.

Exhaustion overcame her, and she desperately needed to be alone to sort out her feelings.

"Marianne, you should know that if you reject Swinton after this, he might sue me for breach of contract.''

"I will speak to him tomorrow," she said noncommittally. Without another word, she fled out of the room and up the stairs to her sanctuary.

Heavy at heart, Leith made his way back toward the Folly. Preoccupied with his problems, he didn't notice Cosmo and Echo Latch at first as they trudged back toward their humble cottage at the bottom of the hill.

"Good evenin', Mr. Sherry," said Cosmo, and doffed his cap.

"Good evenin', Mr. Sherry," echoed Echo.

Leith greeted the two grinning young men. "Did you enjoy the bazaar?"

"Ye can be sure o' that, Mr. Sherry," said Cosmo, and Echo repeated the confidence. "We bought trinkets fer our sister in Ashford."

"Good that the funeral is over, and everything is back to normal," Leith said.

"Ah, 'at's right," Cosmo said. "Ye know, Lady Randome is ever so gen'rous. She gave us new coats fer th' funeral." Hands in pockets, he held out the rough coat until it resembled a tent.

"Splendid." Leith rubbed his chin thoughtfully. "Come to think of it, you helped the midwife lay out the corpse of the earl."

"Aye, that we did," said Cosmo, and "Aye," said Echo.

"Did you perchance find a stack of letters by the dead earl?"

Cosmo folded his round face into thoughtful lines. "When yer mention it, yes, I believe I found some papers on the floor after th' midwife left. I was goin' to give 'em to th' housekeeper, but I furgot."

Leith's hope soared. Perhaps the letters would be

within his grasp in the next fifteen minutes. "What did you do with them, then?"

"Ow, nothin', Mr. Sherry," Cosmo said with maddening calmness. "I believe they're still in th' pocket o' me old coat."

"And where's your old coat?" Leith held his breath.

"Why, I sold it to th' ragman. 'E comes around this area every Tuesday. Gave me sixpence for it, and Echo got sixpence for his."

Echo nodded vigorously, and Leith's hope died. "He won't be back until next Tuesday, then?"

Cosmo shook his head. "Nope. Every Tuesday at eight o'clock in th' mornin' at th' gates." Cosmo gave Leith a close look. "Do ye want t' sell yer coat? A damned waste. Looks fine to me."

"I might want to *buy* one," Leith said sotto voce, and increased his pace. "Good night, gentlemen."

Chapter Twelve

MARIANNE WASHED HER FACE IN COLD WATER THE following morning, trying to relieve the puffiness around her eyes that her lengthy bout of crying had induced. It didn't help much, but at least the shock of the cold water made her wake up.

"Good morning," greeted Miss Dew as she stuck her head around the door. Her eyes widened as she viewed Marianne's ravished face, and Marianne made a grimace.

"What's the matter?"

Marianne sank down on her bed, her shoulders slumping. "Oh, Aunt Annie, I've made a muddle of my life. I don't want to marry Swinton, but now I've said yes. I didn't mean to—I succumbed to his insistent pleas." That last part was a plumper, but Marianne couldn't very well divulge to her chaperon that she'd kissed a butler behind a tree . . . and more. Auntie would be shocked beyond speech; she would blame herself for not doing her duty.

"It's plain as a pikestaff that Swinton is not besotted

137

with you, Marianne, and since you don't want him, you should never have consented to wed him."

"I know. Auntie, I've been such a goosecap. I can barely look at myself in the mirror."

Miss Dew sat down next to Marianne and placed her arm around the young woman's shoulders. "I'll own I'm shocked by your change of mind—concerning Swinton, I mean."

Marianne sighed. "I must speak with him at the earliest moment and tell him that I regret my decision."

"Does this change of heart have any connection to your kissing the Randome butler behind a tree?" Miss Dew looked away, her face embarrassed.

Marianne gasped. "You know?"

Miss Dew nodded. "The squire gave me a rare tongue-lashing last night for not looking after you properly. I feel it's my fault." Her eyes holding a wounded look, she glanced at Marianne. "Why did you do it? Because he's a strapping, young fellow with a contagious grin?"

Marianne took her aunt's hand. She decided she must confide in someone, and Miss Dew would not spread the truth around the village. "Auntie . . . Mr. Sherry is not who he seems to be. In fact, he's not a butler at all, but a member of polite society."

Miss Dew's jaw slacked. "*What* are you talking about? Are you involved in some havey-cavey business that I know nothing about?"

Marianne nodded miserably. "Mr. Sherry is none other than the Honorable Leith Sheridan, of the Longford family."

"The Longfords? Why, they are very influential, a family of the first stare."

"Yes. Leith's grandmother is Antonia, the Dowager

Baroness of Longford." Marianne told her chaperon everything she knew about the love letters. "You see, if the truth would come out that the dowager had a deep *tendre* for the old earl, a scandal would ensue. The letters might be printed in the newspaper for the public to gloat over if the blackmailer doesn't get the eight thousand pounds he demands."

"That's awful." Miss Dew looked as if she was about to fall into a faint. "Utterly hideous."

"So you see why Leith has to keep his identity a secret until he discovers the truth."

Miss Dew pursed her lips in disapproval. "Well, the young man is certainly enterprising. First this business with the letters, then seducing you into kissing him. A harried man, on all accounts."

"I've been such a *fool*," Marianne wailed, with the mortification of knowing she had succumbed to his polished blandishments. Still, she didn't regret kissing him, not for one moment. Once she got over her shame, she would cherish the memory of their short time of bliss. At this point she was sure there would never be more. Not unless Vivian Worton broke off her engagement, and Swinton decided he didn't want to marry after all.

Leith would find the letters, then disappear from the Folly, just like Papa had predicted. A frisson of fear curled down her spine. She would be trapped in Spiggott Hollow forever with only one amorous memory to warm her old age. . . .

"Auntie, you must not tell a soul about this. We must protect the dowager baroness's reputation. It's the honorable thing to do, and I won't have it any other way."

"Mum it is. I respect your decision, Marianne, but you

must admit that Leith Sheridan is touched in his upper works for impersonating a butler.''

Marianne smiled wryly. "Yes, I admit he's a rather inept butler.''

"I mentioned that to Eudora, but she won't hear any of it. She thinks the fellow lends distinction to the Folly. How, I surely don't know. Certainly not with that bushy mustache of his.''

Marianne debated whether to tell her aunt about Leith's betrothal to Vivian Worton, but she decided against it. One shock was enough.

"Well, I shall glance discreetly in some chest of drawers for the letters when I visit the Folly next. A criminal act like extortion should not be happening under Eudora's roof,'' Miss Dew said.

"Lady Randome's too preoccupied with her loss to notice anything around her. One thing is for sure—one of her relatives is badly in needs of funds.''

Miss Dew clutched Marianne's hand. "Besides aiding the Dowager Baroness of Longford, we're doing Eudora a favor if we help Leith Sheridan to find the letters.''

Marianne gave a weak laugh. "I knew you would cast the problem in a positive light. You've always been pluck to the backbone, Aunt Annie.''

"Hmm, it still doesn't explain why Sheridan had to kiss you." She gave Marianne a searching stare. "Is he enamored of you?''

Marianne lifted her shoulders in a shrug. "Who is to say? Only Leith knows the truth about that, but I greatly fear he only wanted a bit of afternoon dalliance with a willing female.'' She wondered if Leith at this very moment was seducing one of the maids behind some door at the Folly.

* * *

Leith's thoughts were aimed in an entirely different direction—how to get out of his engagement to Vivian Worton. Earlier in the morning, he'd said good-bye to Horry Fishborne, who had traveled back to Ashford after a late-night card game in the butler's pantry. Horry, who was always burdened by debt, had demanded one hundred pounds for his silence. Leith had grudgingly paid up, vowing he would win back the money in their next card game. Horry had laughed, calling him a great bounder as he slapped the reins on the backs of his horses.

Bounder, indeed! Leith was supervising the cleaning of the enormous crystal chandeliers in the dining room. Lottie and two of the footmen were perched atop ladders dipping the prisms in a solution of soapy water, then rinsing them off and polishing them with vinegar until they sparkled. Leith had not much to do other than to make sure Lottie didn't fall off the ladder, and that she didn't inveigle the two young men into foolish behavior. Lottie had a knack for creating chaos around her.

Leith glanced out the open French doors to the terrace. The day was sunny and warm, a haze veiling the horizon. Voices and laughter reached his ears, and he walked up to the door, discreetly glancing around the edge of the curtain. To his surprise, he saw Vivian walking arm in arm with Mordecay Follett, chatting amiably, something she had never done with him, Leith thought. All she ever did was berate him for his behavior and other imagined evils.

We would never suit, but how do I tell her that? Leith inserted his finger under his collar, seeking desperately for a solution to this most pressing problem. How could he ever approach Marianne until he'd dissolved his engagement to Vivian? Marianne would never trust him as long as he remained a betrothed man.

"Lei—Sherry, just the man I was looking for," Vivian drawled in the door opening, giving him a vinegary smile. "Please bring a bottle of sherry and some cakes to the rose arbor. I feel quite famished, and so does Lord Randome." She smiled almost sweetly at the earl. It was the first time Leith had seen sweetness in her expression. "We had such an invigorating walk, didn't we, Mordecay?" she said, winding her arm through his once again. "We left Aunt Fulvia far behind."

Leith wanted to pull her inside and explain that she was making a fool of herself, but a *butler* could not take such liberties, and she knew it. "Are you sure you want sherry so early in the morning, Miss Worton?" He viewed Mordecay's brandy-florid face with misgivings. "I could arrange for a glass of lemonade."

"Well, of course we want sherry. Don't be a crotchety old fidget, Sherry, do as I bid, *now*," she said.

Leith found it difficult to bow deferentially. "Certainly, Miss Worton. I shall oblige straightaway."

He returned with a tray, only to find Vivian waiting for him on the terrace. Her eyes were as icy as diamonds. "How long is this charade going to continue, Leith? Have you found the letters?"

He shook his head. "No, but I think I know where they are." He didn't, but he hoped he would find them in Cosmo's old coat, if the ragman still had it among his rags. "However, I do believe now that the blackmailer doesn't know where the letters are. Still, the extortion threats continue. Grandmother has to pay by the end of next week. Not that she will, of course, what with the letters missing, but we can't be too careful."

Her cold gaze swept over his form. "You've trifled with my pride by degrading yourself to a butler. I know you're fond of pranks, but I'll have you know I won't stand for this kind of tomfoolery once we're married. It's humiliating, to say the least."

"You don't have feelings, other than the ones concerning yourself, Vivian," he said just as coldly. "You're only willing to marry me because the union will enhance your status in society. You've never voiced a soft word to me, not even on the day we were betrothed."

Her mouth fell open in shock. "Well! Why should I reveal my feelings to you? Ours is a business transaction, nothing else. You can't pretend to love me."

"Nor you me," he said quietly.

"Really, Leith, don't try to back out of your commitment to me. I shall be your wife just as soon as this debacle is over."

He gave her a hard look. "Meanwhile you make eyes at Lord Randome? It seems to me that you two get on famously. Perhaps you could wed him; an earl would be much more 'elevating' than a mere honorable. Think about that."

Vivian spread her fan and fluttered it before her face. "Don't try to slither out of your contract, Leith. I'll trifle with Mordecay if I please. It's so very tedious here, nothing to do, nothing at all. He helps me pass the time."

"You could always go to London. Grandmother would be as happy as a grig to see you."

Vivian made a moue. "I must keep an eye on you, Leith." She slapped his arm with her fan. "Now come along with that tray. Don't dawdle. Mordecay is thirsty."

Leith swore under his breath, fearing there was no way of getting out of his commitment to Vivian. Somehow he had to find a solution, if his love for Marianne would ever come to its logical conclusion—marriage. After what he'd done yesterday on the bank of the river, he must find a way to atone for his indiscretion. Grandmother would flay him alive if she ever found out that he'd behaved like a veritable twiddlepoop.

Swinton didn't arrive that morning to Darby House, only sent a message that his mother had succumbed to a thunderous headache and needed his attention. Marianne was relieved, yet felt an urge to speak with him, to garner some insight to his plans. The idea of meeting him was daunting, especially since he would feel he was wronged when she kissed Leith. Swinton could hold a grudge, and he would certainly hold it longer than usual this time.

Marianne and Miss Dew set off at eleven o'clock to purchase sewing thread, buttons, and writing material at the local mercantile. The sun was shining, but great rain clouds loomed on the horizon.

"Better hurry before we get soaked," said Miss Dew as they set off, umbrellas clamped under the arms.

At the shop, they met some of the ladies who had baked the pies for the bazaar, and they were soon in the middle of discussing the successful event. "Why, I believe the vicar said we could start replacing the roof before the winter."

"I didn't think we collected that much funds," one lady said.

"I heard a rumor that some generous soul donated a large sum of money toward the repairs. I don't know who. The new earl is not in the line of charity," said another lady.

Marianne's glance shifted to the window. Village gossip held no interest to her this morning. She moved away on the pretext of examining a rack of scarves. The traffic in the high street, mostly farm wagons, rumbled past.

She looked out the window and saw one of the Randome carriages driving through the village with Julia as the only occupant. Evidently Julia was heading toward Darby House. With a wave to Miss Dew, Marianne left the shop and steered her steps homeward.

She saw a lone figure coming out of the Golden Apple across the street. Immediately she recognized Leith Sheridan, his mustache back in place, and his spectacles pinching his nose. Drat the man! she thought uncharitably, and increased her pace, her face averted. Hopefully, he didn't see her.

No such luck. Hurried steps approached her from behind.

"Marianne!" he called out, obviously forgetting his butler role for a moment. "My, you're a sight for sore eyes."

Her heart pounded painfully in her chest. She stopped and faced him. He looked so handsome, so happy to see her, as if he didn't have a care in the world. "Good morning, She—Leith," she said guardedly.

He lowered his voice. "I would dearly like to embrace you right now, but that might be a mistake with so many busybodies watching."

"I seem to recall that we're not on the best of terms," she said.

"Why? Yesterday was the crowning of this wonderful spring. I'd like to see our love go on forever."

"Forever? I strongly doubt that you have any intention of seeing us happy together."

His tender smile diminished. "What do you mean? Everything I said yesterday was true, and I shall approach Squire Darby once I find the letters. I believe I'm close to the solution. The letters might be in Cosmo's old coat.''

Marianne's lips trembled. She wanted badly to believe him, but the matter of Vivian Worton still stood between them.

"Have you already forgotten that the last thing you told me yesterday was that you're betrothed to Miss Worton? Has that little detail already slipped your mind?''

"Of course not," he said heatedly.

"But you're still engaged to her, aren't you?''

He fidgeted, dashing one hand through his hair. "Yes . . . but I'm doing everything I can to get out of the commitment. I just haven't found the best plan of attack yet.''

"Then I would be foolish to hope for your ring on my finger," she said. "Don't you agree?''

"Yes . . . but—''

"Don't 'yes but' me, Leith. Perhaps you could tell Vivian the truth, that you love another woman? That might make her jilt you.''

"Oh, no," Leith said vehemently. "That won't change her mind. If she believes she could humiliate me in some way, she wouldn't hesitate. Vivian is very angry with me for putting off the wedding.''

Marianne gave him a thorough scrutiny. He looked contrite and worried, but how could she trust him as long as he was promised to another? She could find nothing more to say.

He reddened, and his shoulders slumped as if burdened by heavy guilt. "What a pickle," he said, folding his hands behind his back. "Are you very angry?''

Marianne nodded, but the bite of fury she had first

experienced as he confessed to being engaged had softened. "I am, but I'm still barmy enough to hope that you might be speaking the truth."

His face brightened.

"But I still can't trust you," she added, wishing that she could. "You must understand that. I don't think we should speak further, not until you can tell me that you're no longer betrothed."

A farmer's wife and her daughter passed by, staring curiously at Leith and Marianne.

"Yes, it certainly is a lovely day, Mr. Sherry," said Marianne for the benefit of the ladies' ears. "You got my message for the dowager countess? Very well, give her my best as well." She smiled at the farmer's wife and greeted her. In an undertone, she added to Leith, "Good-bye."

"I love you; I always will," he whispered fervently.

"Words are easy to say. I want some tangible proof that you're serious."

"Darling, let me—"

Before he could finish the sentence, Marianne fled back inside the shop to Miss Dew, knowing that due to decorum, he couldn't follow. Still affianced to Miss Worton, she thought, suspecting that he would never find a way to free himself. What if he didn't want to? There was always that possibility. Worry coiled her stomach into a tight knot.

As she returned home with Miss Dew and their purchases, she said, "I spoke with Leith Sheridan."

"I noticed that, as did the rest of the village," Miss Dew said grimly. "The others speculated over what you had to discuss for such a long time with the Randome butler. I hope this won't create unnecessary gossip."

"Well, I might not speak to him again." She glanced

at Miss Dew. "Auntie, I didn't tell you everything. Leith is betrothed to Miss Worton. He said he would find a way out of the engagement, but he has done nothing about it." Misery engulfed her as she voiced those words.

Miss Dew pruned her lips. "I'm shocked! He is a dishonorable young man to bring his fiancée into the charade, and then toy with your feelings. If I were you, I would marry Swinton Langley. Who knows what gossip the villagers might spread about you. It's possible someone besides Swinton saw you kissing the butler. If that becomes common knowledge, you'll be ruined."

Marianne pondered that sad fact as she stepped up to her bedchamber to rest after the midday meal with Julia. She wished she could look into the future and glean some answers.

At three o'clock a messenger delivered a letter to Marianne. She opened it and read:

> *Sorrow fills my heart at the thought*
> *that you might evaporate like the morning mist;*
> *Fear rushes in my footsteps*
> *As I delve into the bleak hollow of my life;*
> *Without you*
> *I cannot live as I cannot embrace the mist.*

Marianne gasped, knowing for sure that Sherry had written the poignant verse—and the previous one. Swinton had lied to her when she'd confronted him at the bazaar.

Tears gathered in her eyes as she folded the note and placed it under her pillow. She would never be able to forget Leith Sheridan.

Swinton arrived at Darby House at precisely four

o'clock, just in time for tea. He helped himself to a buttered scone and two raspberry tarts. Miss Dew went to the kitchen for some fresh cream, and Marianne was left alone with her swain. Squire Darby had been delayed in the stables and would have his tea later.

Swinton looked unusually preoccupied. "What is the matter?" Marianne asked. "You look like it's the end of the world."

"Well, it's Mother. You see, she has the worst headache today. She got up this morning feeling fit as a fiddle, which she hasn't done in a long time. Then I told her."

"What, Swinton?"

"About us, about our upcoming nuptials. I had to tell her, y'see, since we're going to be wed before the week is out."

Marianne swallowed hard in fear. "You haven't spoken to Papa today?"

Swinton gave her a surprised stare. "No, I haven't seen the squire. Why should I speak to him? He's helping me arrange for the special license."

Setting down her plate of scones, Marianne faced her fiancé. Swinton had risen, now walking back and forth across the floor, his hands folded behind him. He wore a stern expression on his face, and spoke in a voice that brooked no nonsense. "We'll soon be wed."

Marianne's voice trembled with agitation. "I told Papa, and I'll tell you now; surely there's no need for such haste. I want us to wait, Swinton. To read the banns takes three weeks, then I want to wait until . . . well, perhaps Christmas for the wedding."

"Christmas? You must have windmills in your head! We cannot wait that long."

"I should think there's no need to travel to Canter-bury," she said, rather more sharply then intended.

"You don't want me to travel to Canterbury? Why this reluctance to accomplish our nuptials? No need to tarry."

Marianne braided her fingers together. "I want the most romantic wedding Spiggott Hollow has seen in this century."

"Fustian! Why would you care to spend a great amount of money on an event that will be over in one day."

Marianne suppressed her anger and schooled her face into complacency. "Why, Swinton, it would be a day to remember for the rest of my life. Wouldn't you like to have such a romantic memory?"

"I don't hold with romantic fiddle-faddle. You ought to know that by now."

"I'm so very disappointed," she said, wondering how she could have been such a fool as to promise to marry him in the first place. Yet there was the matter of the dowager's love letters, and there was the small matter of Vivian Worton standing in the way of true happiness.

Swinton still wore an expression of great agitation.

"You seem overly preoccupied," Marianne said. "I'm sorry if I have offended you in any way."

He shook his head. "My problem doesn't involve you—well, only indirectly. You see, Mother is worried that we won't be happy together, but I tried to allay her fears the best I could." He gave Marianne a placating smile. "She's very fond of you, after all, and knows that you would make a highly suitable companion as her health deteriorates."

Marianne gave a delicate shudder. "Yes . . . she would benefit from a young pair of hands and legs to alleviate her tedium.'' Her voice grew firmer. ''You ought to take her around in the carriage sometime. Take her out to breathe fresh air. A bit of exercise might cure some of her ills.''

His face turned ashen with shock. ''Dear Marianne, I hope you won't suggest that to Mother once you become part of our household. Why, she only goes out once every two months, to the cloth merchant in Ashford for material. She does need some new dresses to cheer her up from time to time.''

''Very sensible of her, of course,'' said Marianne, ''but she could benefit from more than that.''

Swinton raised his hands to plea. ''Don't say another word, dearest.''

''We might as well postpone the wedding. Tell your mother that, and you'll find that she'll recover miraculously.''

Swinton gave her a penetrating stare. ''Do I detect a hint of derision in your voice, Marianne?''

''Heaven forfend! I have your mother's best interests at heart.''

''Hmm.'' He gnawed on the back of his knuckles. ''You might be right. Perhaps we ought to postpone the nuptials for a few weeks, to let Mother get used to the idea.''

Marianne drew a sigh of relief, but she wasn't sure if she'd won any ground by delaying the wedding.

Chapter Thirteen

AT FIVE MINUTES TO EIGHT ON THE FOLLOWING Tuesday, Leith waited in the light morning rain for the ragman to appear at the gate. He finally did, ten minutes late. His wheelbarrow was covered with an old oilcloth, but ragged garments still hung over the sides, getting soaked. With raindrops drumming against his umbrella, Leith halted the ragman with a wave of his hand.

The old man wore a motheaten beaver hat, and a constant drip fell off the rim, down to the filthy front of the fustian jacket, which was soaked through.

"A perishin' day, ain't it, guv?" the ragman said. "Wot d'ye want? A new shirt perhaps? An outfit for the royal court?" He chuckled at his own joke.

"Banter aside, I want two old jackets, the ones Cosmo and Echo sold to you last week."

"Aw, those. Well, only Cosmo sold me 'is. Echo's jacket was naught but great 'oles. I took it off 'is 'ands as a favor."

Leith held his breath in anticipation. "I would like to buy Cosmo's coat from you."

The ragman rubbed his darkly stubbled chin and stared at Leith suspiciously. "Why would a gent like yerself want to buy an ol' tattered coat?"

Leith held out his hand. "It's a matter of great urgency. I'll give you a crown for it."

Bleary blue eyes widened with greed. "Ohhh, I'll say." Then his shoulders slumped. "'Tis my darnedest luck. When a gent is willin' to cough up the dibs, I don't 'ave the merchandise."

"You sold the coat?" Leith's hope fizzled out as if doused with freezing rain.

"Aye, that I did, to a stranger in the village. Never saw 'im afore."

"What kind of stranger?"

The old man scratched his seamed neck. "Wasn't a 'igh-an'-mighty butler like yerself, but 'e wasn't a peasant either."

"Was he a real *gentleman* from London, perhaps?" Leith prodded.

"Oh, no, that he was not. A workin'man, no doubt 'bout that." The old man tipped his brim, water cascading down his long nose. "Good day, Mr. Sherry. I must get a pint inside me before I catch infermentation of the lungs."

"Inflammation . . ." Leith corrected him absentmindedly. No closer to the letters, he returned to the house. Good God, what would Grandmother say when she found out about this? She would come the ugly with him. Unless some transient worker had passed through the village and bought the coat, someone in Spiggott Hollow had the letters. But who? Who would see the letters next? The reverend, or Mr. Langley's mother? In either case, the scandal would be at Grandmother's door.

He confronted Cosmo and Echo at the garden shed

where their supervisor, head gardener Jonas Slocum, was instructing them on how to best plant a hedgerow. Slocum was a squat surly Scot, and Leith had not managed to wring more than five words out of the man since he started working at the Folly.

"Cosmo, come here," Leith demanded, and the twin joined him under the umbrella. "Are you sure the letters were inside that coat you sold to the ragman?"

Cosmo nodded vigorously and squinted at Leith. "Aye, they were. Echo's coat 'ad too many holes in the pockets to 'old anything."

Leith felt burdened by too many obstacles. The letters seemed doomed to be gone forever. "Very well. If you hear anything about their whereabouts, please let me know."

"That I will, guv, and so will Echo." Cosmo saluted and joined his brother. "Echo does everything I arsk him to do."

"Don't tell anyone about our conversation, Cosmo." Leith prayed that he would retrieve the letters before the blackmailer found them.

Later that morning, he sat pondering his situation in the butler's pantry. He ought to do something—try to find the stranger who had bought Cosmo's coat, but that would be a waste of time. It was his half day off, and he needed to find a way to calm his nerves. He had so many unsolved problems to juggle, the most urgent his wobbly relationship with Marianne. He longed for her, longed to hear her voice, see her smile, and drown in her blue-green eyes. Inhaling deeply, he struggled to temper the surge of his yearning. To no avail.

He decided to visit her under the pretext of delivering something to Darby House. From the kitchen he collected a basket of raspberries—when Cook wasn't watching, and sneaked out the backdoor.

Dressed at his most proper, immaculate black coat, linen starched, and neckcloth folded in a simple knot, he stepped through the village. He lifted his hat to acquaintances, stopped at the Golden Apple for a pint of ale to fortify himself, then headed toward the backdoor of Darby House. One day soon he would walk up to the front door, not this furtive creeping around the back.

His heart pounded violently as he knocked. Would she see him? He hadn't as yet been able to convince Vivian that they wouldn't suit.

Cook, her plump arms covered with flour, opened the door. Her eyes widened in surprise. "Why, Mr. Sherry? How do you do? What can I do for you?"

Leith doffed his hat. "Is Miss Darby at home? I have a message for her." He held out the basket. "These are for you. Your associate at the Folly sends her best."

Cook's eyes narrowed in her pudgy face. "Sends her best? Why, that's a surprise, to say the least. We're not on speakin' terms, if ye must know."

Leith cursed himself silently for that blunder. "Perhaps Lady Randome sent them. I can't remember." He gave her a pleading look, and he noticed a maternal light come into her eyes.

"Of course, ye gentlemen have no head for domestic tasks. I'll lay it was Lady Randome who sent the berries. She's ever so thoughtful." Cook apprehended the basket. "If yer lookin' for Miss Marianne, she's in the back garden, weeding." She pointed toward a brick wall that formed a square around the kitchen garden. "In there."

Unchaperoned, Leith hoped as he stepped toward the wrought-iron gate. Inside the wall, the wind could not reach. Vegetables and flowers stretched toward the light, and an abundance of birds chirped in the trees outside the wall. Dressed in a faded muslin gown and an old straw hat, Marianne was on her knees among the perennial flowers.

"Pssst, Marianne," he whispered.

She jerked her head around, her eyes widening in fear. "What are you doing here? If father sees you, he'll throw you out."

"I told Cook I had a message to deliver from Lady Randome."

Marianne's shoulders tensed visibly, and her eyes darkened with distress. "Are you bringing good news? It would be a sad mistake on my part to speak with you if you haven't broken off your engagement to Miss Worton."

He twirled his hat in one hand. "Such big changes don't happen overnight. I have spoken with Vivian, but she's set on marrying me, for the time being."

Marianne threw down her trowel and peeled off her gloves. "If you have no intention of severing your connections to Miss Worton, I don't understand why you have to harass me—in my own home under the eyes of the servants."

Leith glanced around the garden. "They can't see us here."

"Someone might arrive at any minute." She faced him, her expression agitated. "What is your message? If you truly have one."

He glanced away, shifting his weight from one foot to the other. "Yes, I do, but it's not from Lady Randome, it's from me." He dropped his hat and took Marianne's hands between his own. "It's a simple message, but a strong one. I love you."

Her lips started trembling, and her lovely eyes filled

with tears. He reached out to wipe them away, but she pulled her head back. "Do you want me to run off with you as your mistress, is that it? Am I to watch in the crowd as you wed Miss Worton at St. George's?" She tore her hands free. "I *will not* debase myself further."

He noticed the tears glistening in her eyelashes like jewels, and it took all his control not to pull her into his arms. "I knew I would make a muddle of things when I met you and fell in love." His voice softened. "Before you, I truly had never given my heart to anyone."

Marianne laughed, the sound tinged with sadness, but she didn't argue. She heaved a deep sigh, and raised her eyes to his.

He gave her what he believed was a loving smile. It wasn't difficult what with his chest drowning with tender feelings. "My brother, John, was groomed to take on the Longford title. Father put all his faith in John, treating me second best. I was second, but that didn't bother me, other than the fact that I had no direction in life." He sighed. "John did everything as expected of him, married the long-toothed daughter of an archbishop, had four children."

Marianne looked at him more intently, and he sensed he'd touched something in her. "You felt like you were pushed to the side?" she asked.

"Perhaps. Grandmother was the only person who had time to listen to me. I grew up to be a wild buck with nothing but gambling and drinking on my mind. Then Father bought a pair of colors for me and I went to the Continent to fight Boney." He smiled wryly. "I told you before, I received a chest wound. Warring is not for me, I'm afraid. I'm not a seeker of glory."

"You sold out?"

"Yes, and Grandmother was pleased. She's been

trying to find a position for me at some ministry ever since I came back to regain my strength. She's a lady with a mind of her own, and she knows every minister, every admiral, every general. In fact, I think she knows everyone in London.

"Besides my wound, I caught pneumonia. I almost died. However, as I recuperated, I discovered that I could make myself useful in many ways—that I was worth something even though I was only the second son of a baron. Life is too precious to waste on drinking and gambling."

Marianne gripped her hands together. "Why are you telling me about your struggles?"

"I want you to understand that I don't take our love lightly. It's the most serious, the most wonderful thing that has ever happened to me. I'm ready to settle down at my small estate, Fairhaven, in East Anglia, and raise a family—with you." He gave a lopsided smile. "I'm not the libertine you would have me, nor am I a flirt at heart. I can't help that the maids find me attractive, and I can't help that God gave me a devilish smile."

Marianne could not stop herself from laughing. He'd opened up his heart to her, told her about his humiliation, his shortcomings, his growing up. He must be telling her the truth about his feelings.

"You must trust me, Marianne. The doubt in your eyes is breaking my heart."

"I . . . you sent me the love poems, didn't you?" She glanced up into his eyes that were darkened with worry. She hadn't known it then, but the first time he'd greeted her outside the church, those blue, blue eyes had started working their magic on her. She had been lost then, and she was lost now, in love.

"Yes, I will keep sending them as inspiration strikes me, even after we're married."

"They were very sweet, but they don't change the fact that you're still affianced to another lady."

"Let me explain. Father was an old friend of Admiral Worton. The admiral was a lot older than Father. He sired Miss Worton when he was seventy years old. Anyway, he made Father promise to take care of Vivian and make sure nothing would befall her. When Vivian turned eighteen, Father made me promise to marry her. I didn't know Vivian then, and I don't know her very well now. We were engaged, and then Vivian returned to Devonshire, where her home is located."

"She seems to be a lady who knows her own mind," Marianne said. "She will never let you go, especially if she learns that you've visited me today. She'll put two and two together."

"She must see reason. I can't marry her now." Leith pulled Marianne close, burying his face in her sweet-smelling hair. "I love you." All the flower scents of the garden had attached themselves to her, even the pungent smell of damp earth. She felt light in his arms, as elusive as a wood nymph.

"I can't promise you anything, Leith." She tried to pull away, but he couldn't let her go, not just yet. He tilted up her chin and pressed a tender kiss to her soft lips.

"No!" she cried in fear. "Don't try to seduce me in my own garden. Do you want to make a laughingstock out of me?"

"Of course not, but I can't bear to not touch you when you're so close."

She tore away from him, but it was too late. Her eyes widened with horror as she glanced toward the gate.

"Go," she whispered between stiff lips. "Don't dawdle."

He followed her terrified gaze, coming eye to eye with the squire, who was leaning against the gate, elbows resting on the top bar.

He spoke in icy tones. "If you're quite finished, I'd like a word with you, Mr. Sherry." He turned to Marianne. "Daughter, go to your room, and stay there for the rest of the day. It's evident that you're not safe from this *louse* even in your own home."

Marianne gave Leith a pleading glance, then fled into the house through the kitchen entrance. Leith faced the older man, sensing the great wrath directed at him. Marianne's father had every reason to be angry, but after he'd poured out his fury, Leith would speak to him in earnest.

Explode, the squire did, but Leith only listened with half an ear. He concentrated on how Marianne had felt in his arms, how soft her hair, how pliant her lips. Only when the squire mentioned the words "immediate dismissal" did he turn his head toward the older man.

"Yes, Mr. Sherry, you heard me right. I shall report this to Lady Randome and the new earl forthwith. You might as well return to the Folly and pack your bags."

"You don't know me, Mr. Darby," said Leith. "You think I'm a butler when in fact I'm not." He bowed and held out his hand toward the squire. "You must listen to me. I'm Leith Sheridan, resident of London and the estate of Fairhaven, East Anglia." The squire didn't take his outstretched hand, and Leith watched as the color rose alarmingly in the older man's face.

Leith lowered his arm. "I love your daughter, and I hope to make her my wife one day—soon. There are, however, some problems to overcome first."

"Make her your wife? Of all the gall—" The squire sputtered, evidently casting about for a suitably scathing rebuke. "I shall throw you out if you don't leave peacefully." He moved threateningly toward Leith, who realized the squire meant every word. The bull-like man had power in the meaty fists flexing uncomfortably close to his face.

Leith continued, trying to get through the barrier of the other man's fury. "Listen, Squire Darby. I can't give your daughter a title, but I have the funds to provide every luxury for her. First of all I will try to make her happy."

"Happy?" The squire turned purplish, and Leith feared that he would have an apoplexy. "I shall now show you what will make me happy, Mr. Sherry—to throw you out on your ear." He gripped Leith's arm and pushed him out of the walled-in garden.

Leith yanked himself free from the punishing grip. "I shall see myself out," he said angrily.

The squire followed him closely as he skirted the lilacs beside the kitchen path and reached the front gate. "And don't come here with another cock-and-bull story, young man, or I shall set my dogs on you."

Exasperated, Leith faced Marianne's father. "Every word is true! I love your daughter, and I shall prove it."

"I now understand how you've been able to turn Marianne's head, and who knows how many more heads of unsuspecting females. It's all due to an oiled tongue. I'll have you know that I loathe glib Don Juans like you, Mr. Sherry. You're the worst kind."

Leith clenched his jaw to put a stop to his growing wrath. He slammed his hat onto his head. "Good afternoon, Squire Darby."

"Don't you say another word to me," the squire threatened, and locked the gate after him.

Marianne watched from her room on the second floor, hearing every word through the open window. She clutched a sodden handkerchief to her eyes, feeling there would be no end to her tears that day. Her heart seemed to burst when the squire bolted the gate, and she knew she had lost Leith. Even if Miss Worton jilted him, Father would never consent to a marriage between her and Leith Sheridan.

She drew a deep, shuddering sigh as she heard her sire clumping up the stairs to her room. He didn't bother to knock, only flung the door against the wall and marched across the floor to tower over her.

"I thought my eyes had failed me when I watched you and that villainous butler in the garden. Have you completely taken leave of your senses, daughter?"

Marianne cringed at his onslaught, and she took a step back as his wrath poured over her like icy rain. "Well answer me!"

"I know it was a mistake, Papa. I've told Leith that—"

"You believe that faradiddle about his 'other' identity?"

"He is of the Longford family. Lady Antonia Longford is his grandmother."

The squire laughed, a booming sound laced with incredulity. "He's glib, I give him that." He took Marianne's arm and led her to her writing table. "Marianne, oh, Marianne, you're such an innocent. I shouldn't berate you for letting that scoundrel turn your head. I should have him beheaded for pestering you."

"I don't understand," Marianne said. Worry lodged in her throat, and she could barely breathe.

"He's fooled you, don't you see, just to get his own way with you." He pushed her down on the chair in front of the desk. "Now you must write a note to Swinton Langley. I shall send him to Canterbury on the morrow to procure that special license. It's clear that you need the comfort of a husband, just as soon as it can be arranged."

"But, Papa—"

"Don't argue, Marianne. I won't hear another word of protest. With your actions you've proved that your judgment can't be trusted. Now write."

Marianne's hands trembled so much she shook drops of ink all over the paper. "Papa—"

"I won't have it said around the village that my daughter hobnobbed with a butler. A decent butler, like Willow, would not try to seduce an innocent lady."

"Willow is seventy years old," Marianne said with some asperity. She began writing the note to Swinton, but her hand trembled so much she couldn't form the words.

Finally the squire took the quill from her and pulled forth a fresh sheet of paper. With a great flourish he wrote the note and sanded the paper. "There, nothing to it." He folded the missive and sealed it with wax. "I shall see to it that Swinton gets this message posthaste." He patted Marianne's head. "You should be grateful that I care about you. A father wants to protect his daughter from any breath of scandal."

Numb with apprehension, Marianne watched him leave. If a miracle didn't happen within the next day, she would become Mrs. Swinton Langley. She contemplated running away. . . .

Chapter Fourteen

MEANWHILE, THE LATCH TWINS DUG UP AN OLD STUMP at the back of the Folly, quite close to the flourishing strawberry patch. Birds perched on the branches of a huge oak nearby, evidently calculating how large the crop would be. Mr. Slocum had erected a fearsome scarecrow—a head of bristly hay topped with an old hat, hefty arms stuffed with straw raised as if shaking fists at the skies, an old coat, and a red scarf flapping around the scrawny wooden neck.

"Look, Echo," said Cosmo as he straightened and wiped some sweat from his brow with the sleeve of his grimy smock.

"What?" asked the twin, squinting with his good eye.

"I'll be gormed. Mr. Slocum 'as made a scarecrow, an' 'tis wearin' me ole coat."

Scratching his head in consternation, Echo studied the effigy. "'Ow d'ye know it's yer ole jacket?"

"See 'em darned patches on th' sleeves? Mrs. 'Olloway did that for me last Christmas when me elbows were stickin' out in the cold." Cosmo dropped his pickax and ambled over to the strawberry field. "Well, who would 'ave thought a scarecrow would get me coat."

Echo followed, clumping through the strawberry bushes, crushing flowers and emerging berries with his large hobnailed boots.

Cosmo admired the scarecrow. "'E looks better 'an I ever did in that coat. A real gent, if yer arsk me." He touched the broken buttons, then felt inside the pockets. Surprised, he pulled out a thin packet of mangled envelopes tied together with a string.

"Wot's this? Mr. Slocum put a bundle of ol' bills or sumthin' in 'ere." Cosmo scratched his head, and so did Echo. "But why?"

"Wot shall we do with 'em? Burn 'em?" Echo asked hopefully.

"No, ye cawker, we can't burn Mr. Slocum's papers. Wot I don't understand is why 'e would put 'em 'ere." He turned the letters over and over in his hand. "Wus there somethin' I wus supposed to remember 'bout me coat?" he asked Echo, who was picking his nose while contemplating the scarecrow.

"Naw, 'tis jest an' ol' coat. Ye 'ave a new one now," Echo said. "An' I 'ave mine. We must get back to work, or we'll get a tongue-flayin'. That Mr. Slocum is a surly feller."

Absentmindedly Cosmo stuffed the letters into the pocket of his voluminous smock and went back to work.

When Leith returned to the Folly, his thoughts lingering with Marianne and the encounter he'd had with Squire Darby, he noticed a row of coaches on the drive. Evidently the houseguests were taking a drive in the lovely weather. Vivian was sitting very close to Mordecay Follett, who was whispering something in her ear.

Leith wished he were close enough to overhear, but at this point he didn't care what Vivian was doing.

How could he convince the old boar Darby that he truly was Leith Sheridan, and that his intentions toward Marianne were honorable? God, what an imbroglio! As he stepped through the kitchen entrance he came upon Cosmo, laughing with one of the upstairs maids.

"Can you believe it, Mr. Sherry, but Cosmo tells me 'e found 'is ole coat—on the scarecrow in the strawberry field."

Leith's heart lurched, hope filling him. "Your old coat? How is that, Cosmo?"

Cosmo downed the tankard of ale in his hand and wiped his mouth. "Mr. Slocum bought th' coat from th' ragman a week ago for th' scarecrow. Got it almost fer free, 'e told me when I mentioned that the jacket once belonged t' me."

Mr. Slocum—who'd worked at the Folly only two months—must have been a stranger to the ragman, Leith thought. "In the strawberry patch, you said?" he asked, to verify the whereabouts of the damned coat, and dashed down the steps. "I'm going out to look."

"Tell Echo, who's talkin' to that Mrs. Fitz, that I'm goin' down t' the village," he heard Cosmo say as he ran along the path on the side of the mansion. At the corner of the house, he came across Mrs. Fitzwilliam, who half ran, half staggered along the path on wobbly heels.

Leith had to slow down behind her. He couldn't very well hurtle down the path as if a fire were in progress.

He studied her plump back shrouded in black crepe. Wisps of a long chiffon scarf and the ends of the black ribbons adorning her cap whirled in the breeze. She was fluttering her fan as if the breeze wasn't enough to cool her face. Highly agitated, Leith mused, debating whether he should take a shortcut across the rolling lawn. That might look strange, though, the butler dashing through the garden. . . .

Where was the lady heading? he wondered as she veered off toward the vegetable garden and the wide strawberry patch beyond.

Leith slowed his steps, watching her. Excitement rose inside him. Was her errand identical to his? Such a coincidence could not be, or could it? Echo might have told the old lady about the scarecrow wearing Cosmo's coat. *Have I found the blackmailer at last?*

He concealed himself behind a wide-spreading rhododendron shrub and observed her movements. She *was* going to the strawberry patch.

Mrs. Fitzwilliam wended her way along the rows of the strawberry bushes to the middle of the field. Leith held his breath as she approached the scarecrow. She gingerly inserted her hands in the pockets of the coat, felt around, but came up empty-handed. After wiping her palms off with a handkerchief, she unbuttoned the coat and examined the inside pockets. It was her! She had sent those letters to Grandmother.

Leith debated whether to confront her right then and there, but then she might raise hue and cry about his identity. He would have to take his chances.

When she had shaken her hands in revulsion after rebuttoning the coat, Leith stepped forward.

"Mrs. Fitzwilliam, can I help you find something? A bundle of letters perhaps?"

She whirled, her heavy-jawed face blanching. "Sherry? What are you doing here?"

"I saw you heading this way, and I realized that you and I had the same errand. I see you didn't find the letters, so that saves me from looking."

"Letters? I have no idea what you're talking about." She raised her nose in disdain. "I noticed the new addition to the garden, and I wanted to inspect it for myself."

"You inspecting a scarecrow, Mrs. Fitzwilliam?" Leith straightened and took on an air of authority. "I believe you were looking for the letters that you've lost. The ones you've used to blackmail my grandmother, the Dowager Baroness of Longford."

She gave a shriek of outrage, bristling, but Leith could see a whiter tone creeping across her face. "I have not the slightest idea what you're talking about, Sherry. In fact, I shall complain to Lady Randome about your behavior."

"And I shall explain to Lady Randome who I am— Leith Sheridan—and my business here in Spiggott Hollow. Lady Longford is my grandmother, and I will protect her reputation at all costs."

Mrs. Fitzwilliam slid past him, and he couldn't very well apprehend her without the letters to prove her guilt. "I believe you couldn't find the letters, Mrs. Fitzwilliam. I have penetrated your bluff. Without the letters you can't go on extorting money from Lady Longford."

She snorted in derision, and he continued, "If you as much as try to write false ones to continue the blackmail, I'll bring in the law, and you'll be ruined."

"I shall not speak with you any longer, Sherry. It's evident the sun has addled your brain. Get out of my way."

Leith held his ground, walking next to her toward the mansion. "I shall take up the matter with Bow Street in London. . . ."

She slashed her folded fan across his face. "Don't threaten me, young man!"

"Then stop pestering my grandmother. I know you're powerless since you don't have the letters."

She gave him a scalding glare. "Don't take that for granted. I might know where they are." She hurried away from him, rounding the corner of the house and joining the party on the front steps. Leith couldn't very well follow her to the other guests with his accusations, not until he had the letters in his hand.

"Dash it all," he cursed under his breath as he watched her speak with her coachman, who then helped her into the first carriage in the line. The landau took off at the spanking pace.

"Damn and double damn," Leith added to his first curse. He returned to the kitchen, meeting Echo in the doorway.

"Where did Cosmo go, Mr. Sherry?" Echo asked, squinting at Leith.

"He went to the village half an hour ago." Leith barred the twin's path. "Did you speak with Mrs. Fitzwilliam a while ago?"

"That I did." He twirled his hat between his hands. "She 'eard Cosmo speak 'bout some envelopes 'e found in th' pocket of 'is ole coat. Mr. Slocum didn't want 'em. Did ye know that th' coat now—"

Leith gripped the front of Echo's smock. "The letters! What did you do with them?" When Echo only scratched his greasy head in confusion, Leith shook him. "Think!"

"Cosmo took 'em. Per'aps 'e brought 'em 'ome to th' cottage. I don't remember."

Leith lightened his grip. "I'm sorry, Echo, for shouting at you. I must find Cosmo."

"Someone jest said 'e'd gone to the village."

"*I* did," Leith said, exasperated. "Did you tell anyone else about the letters?"

Echo shook his head, strands of hair flying. "Only Mrs. Fitzwilliam. She arsked where we live, so I tole 'er."

"Oh, no!" Leith said, and catapulted down the steps. He must get to the cottage before the old harpy.

Meanwhile Marianne and Miss Dew were talking to Cosmo in the street outside the Golden Apple. In her hand, Marianne held a basket of pastries that she was going to deliver to a sick neighbor. Miss Dew—under the strictest orders not to let Marianne out of her sight—had made her charge go out into the sunshine even though Marianne only wanted to bury her head under her pillow and cry. This afternoon Swinton was going to Canterbury, and by tomorrow night she would be Mrs. Swinton Langley. Marianne quaked at the frightful thought.

"Imagine, Miss Marianne," Cosmo said, "isn't it strange that Mr. Slocum bought me ol' coat and put it on th' scarecrow?" Cosmo scratched his lanky hair under the greasy rim of his hat. "It wusn't *that* ragged of a coat."

Marianne listened with rising amazement. "Well, at least it came to good use. Think about it, the birds won't eat all the berries when they are ripe. I'm sure Cook will give you more strawberry tarts than you can eat."

"Hmm, I hadn't figgered that."

Marianne suddenly remembered Leith's letters, which supposedly had disappeared with the coat. She glanced at Miss Dew, whose face bore an expression of suspicion. "Don't get involved in Mr. Sheridan's affairs. 'Tis too late for that now," her aunt whispered.

Marianne paid no heed to Miss Dew's warning.

"Cosmo," she said, "did you find a stack of letters in the pocket of your old coat?"

Cosmo looked confused, then his brow cleared as if by magic. "O' course, that wus the thing I wus supposed to remember! The bundle was thin, sort o' stuck to the lining o' the pocket. I wus to give 'em to Mr. Sherry, but I forgot."

"Where are they now?" Marianne asked, holding her breath.

"Why, I believe I left 'em at 'ome. I didn't want to cart 'em around in me pocket like."

Marianne beckoned with her hand. "Let's go and find them. We can give them to Mr. Sherry later."

"Don't bother with this," hissed Miss Dew, to deaf ears. "You will only get into another pickle, and the squire will be furious."

"Oh, botheration," said Marianne. "The squire won't find out. Let's just say we're doing this for the Dowager Lady Longford."

Marianne and Miss Dew had to run to keep up with Cosmo's giant steps. He swung his arms and whistled a ditty as he led them up high street toward the bottom of the hill on which the Folly sat. A tall privet hedge separated the twins' property from the lane. The old cottage had a sagging thatched roof and wattle-and-daub walls. Hollyhocks with clusters of red and yellow buds stood sentinel on each side of the door. A striped cat sunned itself on the front steps, then slunk behind a shrub as the trio marched up the front path.

The rattle of a coach sounded in the lane outside.

"Me 'ouse," said Cosmo proudly, "and Echo's, o' course. 'Tis not often we get such el'vated company."

Marianne viewed the low-ceilinged room, thinking that what Cosmo and Echo needed most was a charwoman. Dust lay in thick layers on every flat surface, and dirty dishes were stacked on the table. Among an assortment of old food, a stale piece of cheese, a hunk of hard bread, and the smelly residues of a fish pie, Marianne spied a stack of letters. The envelopes were soiled, the ribbon around them frayed.

"Are those the letters that Mr. Sherry wanted?" Marianne asked, pointing at the stack.

"The same," Cosmo replied, nodding vigorously. He scooped them up and gave them to Marianne. "Do you think I should give 'em to Mr. Sherry, or—"

"I could do it for you," Marianne offered.

The sound of a carriage halting on the gravel outside reached their ears.

"Are you expecting company, Cosmo?" asked Marianne.

He cocked his ear to one side. "Naw, I don't know an'one wi' such a fine wagon."

Marianne glanced out the window and noticed the Randome crest on the door immediately.

"Someone from the Folly. Who could that be visiting you, Cosmo? Perhaps there's a message for you."

Cosmo pushed his hat back and scratched his forehead, the confused look returning to his face. "Why . . . what? Message? I don't un'erstand."

Marianne watched with rising curiosity as Mrs. Fitzwilliam stepped down, unaided, and fluttered toward the door, which was partly open. She gave a peremptory knock on the door frame. "Mr. Latch, are you there?"

Cosmo stepped hesitantly toward the door. "Ye want me, Mrs. Fitz?" Worried, he swept off his hat and opened the door wide. He twirled the brim around and around in his work-roughened hands, and Marianne watched as he paled with awe.

Mrs. Fitzwilliam swept inside, then stopped abruptly as she came face-to-face with Marianne and Miss Dew. Her eyes darkened in anger. "You! What are you doing here, Marianne?"

By instinct, Marianne hid the letters in the folds of her dress. "I could ask the same of you, Mrs. Fitzwilliam. I didn't know you were friendly with the Latch twins, but then again, everyone in the village knows and likes them."

Mrs. Fitzwilliam tilted her nose up. "I have no business with them, not after today anyway." She turned to Cosmo. "I would dearly like to have the letters you found in your old coat. Echo said they were here. I'm willing to pay for them handsomely."

Cosmo screwed up his face in consternation. "You, Mrs. Fitz? But . . . but Mr. Sherry asked that I give 'em to 'im if I found 'em."

"They are not his," Mrs. Fitzwilliam said angrily. "Now hurry up, I don't have all day." She gave Marianne a hard stare. "I suppose you wonder what I want with a bundle of old letters. It's family business. The letters once belonged to Lord Randome. They should be returned to their rightful place—the Folly."

"You're the one," said Miss Dew, glaring accusingly at Mrs. Fitzwilliam.

"You're the one who has been blackmailing the Dowager Lady Longford, aren't you?" Marianne filled in. "Why else would the letters matter to you? Why else would you be here now?"

She noticed the infinitesimal backward step that Mrs. Fitzwilliam took at the mention of the Longford name. "Family honor, you know," the older lady said lamely.

"Lord Randome should be here to defend the family

honor, not you," Marianne said. "I believe you're lying."

Mrs. Fitzwilliam's face twisted with wrath, and her eyes expressed a flash of cunning. "I don't care what you believe. I shall have those letters *now!*"

"A shame on you, Mrs. Fitzwilliam. How could you do such a dastardly thing?" Miss Dew berated, shaking her finger. "Extorting money from a defenseless old lady—"

"Defenseless?" Mrs. Fitzwilliam snorted. "Lady Longford is powerful, and she has had her grandson to run her errands for her. He told me so himself, today."

"Grandson?" Cosmo mumbled, scratching his head wildly. "Why would a nipper run errands fer a Lady Londonford at th' Folly? That ol' crow must be some corkbrain."

"Cosmo, don't you dare to slander Lady Longford's name," admonished Miss Dew.

Cosmo raised his bearlike shoulders. "I'm only trying to help."

"Now give me those letters, and don't drag your feet, Cosmo."

Cosmo twirled his hat in agitation. "I don't 'ave 'em, Mrs. Fitz. I gave 'em to Miss Darby. She'll know what t' do with 'em."

Marianne hid the letters deeper in her dress folds and gazed around the small room that was a combination of kitchen and living room. The fireplace was next to the dry sink, and Marianne sidled toward it. Mrs. Fitzwilliam would not get the letters.

"I shall tell Squire Darby I saw you kiss that infernal butler at the bazaar," Mrs. Fitzwilliam threatened. "Give me the letters. I shall tell the entire village, and your reputation will be ruined."

Marianne hesitated, knowing that the threat was real. Even if she married Swinton, her reputation might be destroyed. Swinton would never forgive her. She pulled out the letters and looked at them sadly. What was more important? Swinton and her reputation, or her love for Leith Sheridan, and his grandmother's reputation?

As she hesitated Mrs. Fitzwilliam lunged for the bundle in her hand. Marianne managed to avert the attack, snatching them out of the reach of Mrs. Fitzwilliam's greedy fingers.

"I will show you what wrath is," the older woman threatened, the black scarf fluttering like bat wings around her as she spread her arms wide. She held up her folded fan as if ready to strike down on Marianne's arm.

Miss Dew screeched in anger and pushed Mrs. Fitzwilliam in the back, so that she staggered forward. She caught herself on the back of a chair, and Marianne moved away.

She glanced at the fireplace, noting vaguely that heat was still rising from the embers. A faint glow shone among the ashes under trivet and kettle.

Shouts and pounding footsteps drifted through the door, and there Leith was, eyeglasses askew, mustache half-gone. Perspiration was streaming down his face and his hair hung in tangled curls over his brow.

"Where . . . are the damned . . . letters?" he demanded while trying to catch his breath.

Cosmo shrunk against the wall, his mouth gaping. Pale, he raised a trembling finger toward Marianne. "She's got 'em, Mr. Sherry."

Mrs. Fitzwilliam made another attack on Marianne who fell to her knees, still holding the letters. As Miss Dew struggled to pull off the heavy Mrs. Fitzwilliam, Marianne tore the old papers in two with an enormous tug, and dragged herself across the floor another yard. Mrs. Fitzwilliam hung on to her legs, but she reached the fireplace. She pushed the pieces into the glowing embers, burning her fingertips in the process.

Leith, evidently having understood the situation, grabbed Mrs. Fitzwilliam under the arms and hauled her upright. "I shall take you to the local jail and report you to the police."

Mrs. Fitzwilliam crumbled with a moan as she watched the letters curling up, edges browning, then flaring into flame. "Oh, no, everything is lost," she wailed, and sank down onto a chair. She clawed blindly into her reticule for a handkerchief as great tears filled her eyes.

With Leith's help, Marianne struggled to her feet. She blushed as she witnessed the love and gratitude in his eyes. He held her shoulders in a tight grip, but when Miss Dew stepped forward with a grim expression on her face, he relinquished his grip.

"Thank you," he whispered.

"I could not have done differently."

"You'll pay for this, Miss Darby," said Mrs. Fitzwilliam darkly from behind her handkerchief.

"*You* shall pay, Mrs. Fitzwilliam," said Leith.

"You should be ashamed of yourself, Mrs. Fitzwilliam," said Miss Dew.

"I don't understand—" said Cosmo, his gaze darting from one face to another. "Wot are ye arguin' about?"

Marianne said nothing, only gazed with longing at the gentleman she loved. Perhaps it would be the last time she would see Leith's handsome face and affectionate grin. After tomorrow he would be lost.

"Come, Marianne," said Miss Dew, and grabbed her

wrist. "Let's leave now that we've accomplished what we came here to do."

Mrs. Fitzwilliam gave them a venomous look. "I will ruin you, Miss Darby!"

Leith leaned over the old lady and shook his head. "You must take back your threat this minute, or I shall have you hauled to the jail in public. I hear that the cells are full of rats and other unspeakable things left behind by murderers and pickpockets."

Mrs. Fitzwilliam blanched, pressing her handkerchief to her mouth to stifle a moan. "Oh, you can't do that, Mr. Sheridan."

"I can and I will," he said. "Apologize to Miss Darby and Miss Dew this instant, and I might let you go."

Marianne gasped. He would let Mrs. Fitzwilliam go without punishment?

Silence grew in the room as the ladies viewed each other uneasily.

"Oh very well," spat Mrs. Fitzwilliam. "I won't say anything to spoil Miss Darby's reputation."

"Why in the world did you do such a feather-witted thing as to blackmail my grandmother?" Leith asked, still looming over Mrs. Fitzwilliam as if he was afraid she would bolt to the door.

The plump shoulders sagged under her dark gown. "I—you don't know what poverty I am facing," she explained in a broken voice. "I had hoped that my brother, Egbert, would leave me and Virgil something in his will. He told me before he died that he'd given us *nothing*. You see, he didn't get along with Virgil, called him a namby-pamby and a gamester."

"Your son gambles quite extravagantly," said Leith. "But I thought you were well provided for by your late husband."

"Hah! That unfeeling idiot left us a mountain of debts, nothing else. We've lived on credit for the last year and what small amounts my Virgil might win at the tables." She heaved a shuddering sigh. "It's been a horrid time, and I don't see an end to my problems."

"Surely the new earl might share some of his bounty," Leith said. "Have you asked him? It appears that Virgil and he are good friends. You must throw yourself at his mercy."

Marianne doubted that Mordecay would find much generosity in his heart, but surely he wouldn't let his relatives starve. She felt a stab of pity for the old woman who had been pushed to crime for survival. Yet Mrs. Fitzwilliam had no thought for the people she had hurt in the process.

"Very well, since the letters are now gone, you don't have any reason to pressure my grandmother." Leith straightened with a sigh. "If you as much as try to pester her again, I shall personally see to it that you receive proper punishment." He turned around and escorted Marianne out the door.

Cosmo was outside, waiting. "Could someone 'xplain wot's goin' on in me own 'ouse," he pleaded.

Leith laughed and pulled a gold sovereign from his pocket. "You found the letters, Cosmo. That was all I needed. You've been of great help." He tossed the coin to Cosmo, whose face lightened with a grin.

"I like to be o' service anytime, Mr. Sherry."

"It's good he didn't understand everything," Leith said under his breath, and Marianne laughed.

Leith tugged at her arm, and Miss Dew tugged at her other arm. "We must return home, Marianne. If your father discovers that you've been closeted in the Latch cottage with Mr. Sheridan, he'll fly into the boughs."

"Why did you let her go without punishment?" Marianne asked.

"Well, I didn't want to rake up the matter of Lord Randome's and my grandmother's love letters. The love story would become public if I were to take Mrs. Fitzwilliam to court. Anyway, she's not really a criminal, only desperate."

"It worked out for the best," said Miss Dew with some asperity. "Best shy away from notoriety. Now come along, Marianne." She tugged harder at Marianne's arm.

Marianne exchanged a heated glance with Leith, and her heart thumped wildly against her ribs. "It's no use, Leith. Tomorrow I will become Mrs. Swinton Langley. He's procuring a special license this afternoon, and I have no right to go against my father's wishes."

"I have no compunction going against the squire, but it will be difficult to convince him that we're made for one another."

Marianne felt a faint stirring of hope. "Then Miss Worton has broken off the engagement?"

Leith shook his head. "No . . . but I'll go back to the Folly right now—"

"Don't bother," Marianne said sadly. "I shan't listen to your blandishments any longer. Good-bye, Leith." She ran ahead of Miss Dew, wondering if there ever was a cure for a broken heart.

Chapter
Fifteen

SINCE HE DIDN'T WANT TO BE NOTICED WITHOUT HIS mustache, Leith sneaked into the Folly through a side door. He debated whether to divulge his true identity to Lady Randome but decided against it. The less known about the love letters, the better. He was sure Mrs. Fitzwilliam would keep her mouth shut to conceal her own involvement in the sordid business.

The letters were gone, and thank heaven for that, Leith thought, kicking up his heels in satisfaction. Grandmother would be at peace.

He entered the butler's pantry and rooted through the contents of his shabby chest of drawers for another set of mustache pieces. He found them, noting that they were slightly darker than the previous pair. Hopefully no one would notice. After today, he didn't care. He would speak with Vivian, *beg* her to let him out of their contract. Then he would leave his position at Randome's Folly.

He glued the mustache into place and changed his shirt. His exertions at the cottage had rumpled that garment beyond repair. After donning his coat and the proper dignified expression of a first-rate butler, he headed toward the servants' hall. Lottie met him with a smile and the message that he'd received a letter with the morning post.

Wondering who had written to him, he took the letter and went back to his den—out of view of nosy maids. He glanced at the envelope and recognized his grandmother's handwriting. Apprehensive, he read the missive.

Dear Grandson,
    I have been worried sick about you, suspecting that I have sent you on a mission that might ruin all our lives. Since I haven't heard from you in a week, I've decided to pay Spiggott Hollow a visit. You told me the local inn is called the Golden Apple. Meet me there at three o'clock on Monday the twenty-sixth.

                                                            Antonia

Leith glanced at his turnip watch. *Today,* she's coming today, in two hours. At least he had good news to report. He crumpled the letter and tossed it into the fireplace. Since that matter was out of the way, he only had one more confrontation at the Folly, and he feared he would not be as easily victorious in that battle.

Clenching his jaw and easing the pinch of his neckcloth with his finger, Leith went in search of his fiancée. From the terrace, he saw that she was in a group having a picnic by the pond. He'd better approach her with a note, rather than demanding an interview, which would look odd. He scrawled a message on a piece of paper on the earl's desk:

Vivian, please see me right now in the study, Leith.

He folded it with a flourish. Placing it on a silver salver, he made his dignified walk to the group.

He noticed Mrs. Caldway and Mordecay Follett, the vicar, Lady Fulvia Worton, and Vivian. There was no sign of Mrs. Fitzwilliam and her son. They must have left in a hurry. He approached Vivian, who gave him a glare.

"Miss Worton, a message for you," he said with a stiff bow.

She frowned, scrutinizing his face. Without a word, she unfolded the paper. Leith turned and walked back to the mansion, waiting in the study for her to make her excuse at the table.

She swept inside two minutes later, her skirts making an impatient swishing sound. "This had better be important," she said. "I had to fabricate a lie to keep this appointment."

Leith folded his arms, waiting until her tirade had stopped. "I have finished my mission," he explained. "The letters have been destroyed."

Her face brightened. "That means I no longer have to move around in mortal fear that your deception will be discovered?"

He nodded. "I shall leave the Folly this evening and return to London. However, there's a matter I want to clarify." He took a deep breath, scanning her face where a forbidding frown was taking shape. "It's about our betrothal."

"What about it? You look like you've eaten a lemon, Leith." She hunched her shoulders defensively.

"I . . . you . . . well, I really don't think we would suit, Vivian. I've told you before." When she didn't answer, he continued. "I will, of course, do the honorable thing and marry you like I promised, but I must be frank. Father demanded that I offer for you, Vivian. I didn't do it out of love. To put it baldly, I have given my heart elsewhere."

She gasped and clapped her hand to her mouth. "You truly want me to jilt you—as you are rejecting me now?"

Leith found that his palms were damp. Was it too late to make Vivian see reason, or had it always been too late for him and Marianne? "I'm honest with you, just like I would like you to be honest with me."

"You're putting me in a very awkward position, Leith." She stared at him from under a wide sweep of eyelashes. "I take it you've given your heart to Marianne Darby? She's the only eligible female in these parts."

He nodded mutely, wondering if Vivian would grow spiteful and shower Marianne with her resentment.

Vivian paced the room, chewing on her fingernails. "I will have you know that I'm not wholly without admirers—even though I am betrothed to you."

"You're a regal lady," said Leith, adding silently, *if a trifle high in the instep.* He prayed that she would give him his freedom. "Gentlemen are bound to admire you."

She finally placed her hands on her hips and said, "I don't like this one bit! If you think you can make eyes at Marianne Darby while being engaged to me, you're sadly mistaken. You must see that, Leith. I will not discuss this matter further, and you shall fulfill your promise to me. It's the right thing to do."

Leith's spirit plummeted. As he'd suspected, there was no reasoning with Vivian. She had set her eyes on his fortune—for her own security, and she would hold him to his promise whether he loved her or not.

"What is going on?" asked Mordecay from the door opening. He was holding a pastry in one hand and a glass of wine in the other. "I came in search of you, Miss Vivian." He gave Leith a cold stare. "Is Sherry bothering you?"

Leith bowed. "If you permit me to speak, Lord Randome, Miss Worton was giving me instructions about her trunks. I believe she's returning to London this evening."

"But you can't do that," Mordecay cried, chewing rapidly. "I'll be desolate rambling around this old mausoleum without you, Viv."

Vivian's eyes shot fire at Leith. "Perhaps I must go. Aunt Fulvia and I have been here long enough. Life must go on."

With those words she sped outside, and Mordecay sprinted after her. With a heavy sigh, Leith left the room. He had no choice but to marry Vivian.

An hour later he rushed into the Golden Apple. To drown his sorrow and disappointment, he drank three glasses of claret in rapid succession. The proprietor made some comment about "exhausting work at the Folly" and winked. Leith could not force a smile. He felt as if shrouded in dense rain clouds, inside and out.

When the creak of steel springs and the rapid clatter of hoofbeats reached his ears, he downed the rest of the wine and went outside. Sure enough, before the carriage itself came into view, Leith recognized the horses. They were almost as old as Grandmother, Leith thought with a glimmer of a smile, their coats liberally sprinkled with gray hairs. The coach pulled up only long enough for Leith to jump inside. If he wanted to keep his Sherry identity intact, it would not do to be seen hobnobbing with gentry in the village.

"Leith, my dear boy!" the dowager cried, throwing the dangling ends of her ubiquitous muffler over her shoulders.

Leith chuckled and leaned over to kiss her papery cheek. "I've missed you, Grandmother."

She patted his head, her eyes gleaming. "I've missed you, too, Leith."

The coachman halted the horses by the side of the road a mile outside the village. The dowager opened her fan and began fluttering it in front of her face. "You must tell me all the news. I'm bursting with curiosity."

Leith rubbed his hands. "I've finished my mission. The letters are destroyed—burned."

Her eyes widened, then filled with pleasure. "I say! Well done, my boy. Tell me, who was blackmailing me?"

"Mrs. Fitzwilliam, the earl's sister. It appears she has not a feather to fly with."

"Oh, dear me, just imagine that a person can fall so low."

Leith nodded. "Yes, I believe she was desperate. However, you won't be bothered by her any longer. I threatened her with rat-infested dungeons and a public trial."

The dowager crowed, tossing her scarf this way and that way. "I'm delighted. Now tell me all about it."

Leith launched into the story of the missing letters, Cosmo's coat, and Marianne's brave actions in the cottage. Sorrow clutched his heart as he mentioned her name.

"Miss Darby certainly had her wits about her," said the dowager. "I'm grateful to the gel."

"Yes . . . she's the kindest, the most honorable person I've ever met. And the most charming." He fell into the memories of her blue-green eyes and her silky golden hair.

The dowager tsk-tsked. "If I didn't know you better, I'd say you're in love, my boy."

Leith started, meeting the dowager's disconcerting blue gaze. He flushed, knowing that she could read his very soul.

"Grandmother, I believe you're right on that score," he said, mortified.

She gave a whoop of mirth that startled the horses. They trampled the ground, snorting, and the dowager erupted in a heartfelt "Hurrah!"

"Grandmother!" Leith admonished, casting a surreptitious glance out the window.

"In love at last!" The dowager quieted, her keen eyes never leaving Leith's face. "I have waited for years for that to happen." She pursed her lips. "It's obvious that the lady who has claimed your heart is not Vivian Worton, but Miss Darby."

Leith nodded. "Yes . . . but Vivian is at the Folly, thanks to you. She's very angry with me." Leith explained how he'd tried to break off with his fiancée. "She won't let me go. I want to marry Marianne Darby, and *she's* engaged to another. In fact, she'll be wed by tonight and bundled off to live in a sagging mansion with a hypochondriac for a companion."

"Oh, my, what a muddle you've made of things, Leith." The dowager snapped her fan shut. "It's clear that I'll have to take the matter in hand. I shall pay Vivian a visit. You go to Miss Darby and make sure to stall her wedding ceremony. She's not going to marry anyone but you."

"Grandmother, I don't see how you can make any progress with Vivian when I failed. She's stubborn as a mule, set on marrying me no matter what."

The dowager cackled and swung one end of her scarf at Leith's face. "Don't underestimate me, grandson."

On those words, they returned to the village. Leith jumped down by the common, right beside the Darby property. He didn't know what to do next. Squire Darby would throw him out on his ear if he as much as set a foot across the threshold of Darby House.

Come now, he told himself. Where's your gumption? If Grandmother dares to take on Vivian Worton, I dare to take on that bull of a man. Emboldened by that thought, he ripped off his mustache and his glasses, straightened his neckcloth and his coat, and steered his step toward Darby House.

Marianne waited in apprehension for Swinton Langley to return with the special license. Father had already sent a message to the vicar to appear at six o'clock for the nuptials. Marianne could not recall a time when she'd felt more despondent, except for the day when her mother died. Losing Leith was almost harder because she knew he would be living somewhere out of reach, at the side of his wife.

She could hear her father stomping into his study below. He was still angry with her for becoming involved in an illicit romance with a man he believed to be a butler.

Marianne went to the window and parted the chintz curtains. The sunlight slanted across the common, a golden haze mellowing the fierce green of the field. She saw a man crossing the grass, his stride purposeful. He was tall and broad-shouldered, and he held his head high. She knew only one man with that aristocratic bearing and that wavy chestnut hair. Leith Sheridan, and he was heading toward the front door of Darby House.

She hurried across the room to get a glimpse of Leith as he walked up to the entrance. Struggling to open the window, she could hear him apply the knocker. She leaned out, whispering his name, "Leith!" It wouldn't do for the squire to hear her in conversation with the "villainous butler" as he so scathingly called Leith.

"Pssst," she continued, louder this time. He took a step back and looked up past the lintel.

"Marianne," he said, his troubled face brightening with a tender smile. "I can't get you out of my mind. I've come to talk some sense into your father."

Her heart ached with love. "That'll be a rough undertaking. Father will beat you, I know he will. I don't want you to get hurt."

He shook his head. "I'll make him see reason, don't you worry."

"He has locked me in my room. I can't get out and plead for you."

At that moment the front door opened, and Marianne could hear Willow's scandalized voice. "Mr. Sherry? You're at the front door! You'd better go around back."

"I'm here to see Squire Darby, and I certainly won't go around back to see him."

Willow was quiet for a moment. "S-squire Darby? Well, I say." His tone of voice turned decidedly chilly. "The squire gave me orders that you were not to be admitted at any time."

Marianne waited with bated breath for Leith's response. "If you don't let me in, I'll kick down the door."

Willow gasped. "Come along, then, but I hope I won't lose my position for letting you into the house."

Marianne admired Leith for his daring, but she feared for his fate. The squire wasn't above doling out a few blows to the jaw if he was provoked. He had always taken a great interest in pugilism and still went to watch fistfights.

Evidently Willow hadn't had time to close the front door. As Marianne hung halfway outside her window she heard her father's booming voice in the hallway.

"Willow, what is that varmint doing here?"

"S-sir . . . I don't know," said Willow.

"Throw him out."

"*Sir,* I'm hardly the man to do that."

"Willow is right. I'm a head taller and several stone heavier, not to mention forty years younger," drawled Leith. "If someone is to be thrown out, you'd better do it yourself, Squire Darby."

"Hmm, are you pining for a scuffle, young whelp?"

Marianne drew in her breath sharply in fear. "Leith, don't fight," she cried, hoping he could hear her. She didn't care if the squire got angrier with her. He was already at explosion point.

"No, I didn't come here to get involved in a brawl, but if that's what it takes to make you listen, then by God, let's—"

The squire interrupted him with a bellowing laugh. "I have met coxcombs in my day, but you certainly take the prize."

"You may say what's on your mind, but I promise you won't have the last word," Leith said icily, and Marianne clutched the window frame until her knuckles ached.

She heard the start of a skirmish, feet stomping, groans, a sickening thud. Staggering backward, Leith entered her view. He went down the steps and onto the lawn, the squire following with his sleeves rolled up and meaty fists bunched. Leith tossed off his jacket and took a position of defense.

Marianne moaned as her father let out a shout and pounced on Leith with a left hook. The younger man averted the attack and gave the squire a series of hard jabs on the shoulder.

"You young whippersnapper," growled the squire.

"Papa, don't hurt him," Marianne shouted. "Please stop."

"Don't worry, dearest," Leith said between labored breaths. "You won't have to marry Langley. I'll see to that."

The squire laughed and delivered a stunning blow to Leith's face. Marianne squeezed her eyes shut, but opened them again when she heard Leith swear and lunge at her father.

"I shall talk some sense into you, Squire Darby," he said, dancing around the heavier and slower adversary. "Miss Marianne shall marry me in due time—once these bruises fade." He staggered back as the squire's fist struck his eye. "She won't marry that toad—" Any more epithets were stuffed right back into his mouth as the squire delivered an uppercut that rattled Leith's teeth. Marianne bit down on her knuckle so as not to scream.

A furious gleam lightened Leith's eyes. "She's going to marry . . . me . . . me," he said somewhat groggily. "I'm not Sh-Sherry." He staggered as if drunk as the squire doled out another blow. "I'm the Hon . . . Honorable Leith . . . Sh-Sheridan." He delivered a heavy swinging blow, sending the squire sprawling on his backside. Leith sank down to his knees, blood running from his nose and dripping onto his pristine shirtfront.

"Are you satisfied now, Papa?" Marianne cried angrily. "Why won't you ever listen? He's speaking the truth."

The squire stood with his sturdy arms hanging limply at his sides. With a heaving chest, he watched the younger man struggle to his feet. "Have you had enough, brazen butler?" Squire Darby spat, and Marianne realized that he still didn't believe in Leith.

An old coach came at high speed along the lane and drew to a halt at the gates. Marianne squinted against the glaring sunlight at the horses. She didn't recognize the equipage. The coachman, dressed in outmoded livery, tooled the team through the gates and up the drive. The door flew open and out stepped a diminutive lady in an old-fashioned black dress and a striped wool muffler around her neck. Her hair was a cap of flyaway gray curls, and a purple ostrich plume waggled in solitary splendor on the top of her head.

"What in the world!" the lady exclaimed, and held a quizzing glass to her eyes. "What is going on here?" She stepped up close to the squire and glared at him, then shook one bony finger under his nose.

Marianne watched, breathless. Without introduction, she knew this was Leith's grandmother. There was a likeness about the nose and the chin, and the proud bearing he had certainly inherited from her.

"Grandmother," Leith said, straightening up and rolling his shoulders.

The Dowager Lady Longford held out a minuscule lace-edged handkerchief toward him.

"Wipe your nose, Leith. Blood makes me squeamish."

Leith scowled at the scrap of fabric in her hand and pushed it back. From his pocket, he hauled a much more serviceable square and pressed it to his mauled nose.

"I demand to know why you have rearranged my

grandson's face!'' the dowager said to the squire, and gripped his earlobe. ''And the truth, please.''

''Grandmother,'' Leith began, but he was interrupted by a loud snort from the squire as he pulled free from the dowager's punishing grip.

''And who might you be?'' Marianne's father asked, staring at her outlandish garments. ''An escapee from Bedlam?''

''Father!'' Marianne cried in the window. ''Don't—''

The dowager rapped the squire's arm with her fan. ''Now listen here, young man! That is no way to speak to a lady. I think you're the rudest man I've ever encountered.''

Marianne giggled nervously. No one had ever called her father a ''young man,'' not since he grew a paunch and a jowly face. The dowager must be ancient.

The squire placed his hands on his hips and stared down at the tiny woman in front of him. ''I resent strangers driving up and telling me I'm rude.''

''Father, this must be Lady Longford, Sher—Leith's grandmother.''

The squire's jaw slacked. ''Lady Longford? That's a plumper if I ever heard one.'' He pointed toward Leith. ''If you're related to this rapscallion, I suggest you haul him—and yourself—away in that contraption in which you arrived.''

Leith gave Marianne a wink, and she calmed down. His eyes promised he wasn't going to leave her to face her father's wrath alone.

''Contraption? Well, you're a rudesby and an ignorant.'' The dowager bristled, shaking her fist at the squire. ''I'll have you know that's a first-rate carriage.''

''Father, please don't quarrel any longer,'' Marianne begged.

Leith took the dowager's arm and pulled her to a safe distance from the squire, right below Marianne's window. He looked up, urging his grandmother to do the same. "Look, Grandmother, there's the lady I want to make my wife."

The dowager angled her quizzing glass at Marianne, who blushed. "Lovely creature," said the old lady in an approving voice. "Looks kinder than Vivian."

"By the way, where is Vivian?" Leith demanded to know.

The dowager snorted. "Wouldn't you know, she has eloped with the young Earl of Randome. Fulvia was beside herself with shame at such wanton behavior. I could have told her that Vivian always had a devious side to her character."

Leith gave a whoop of delight. "*Eloped?* By Jove, that's the best news I've had in a long time."

"I think that Fulvia—behind all that hand-wringing and moaning, was pleased with Vivian's match. After all, an earl is a better catch than a mere honorable."

"I told Vivian that, but she wouldn't listen," Leith said.

The squire peered from Marianne to Leith to the dowager. "This is the outside of enough! I don't want to hear any more cock-and-bull stories today."

"Father, please let me out. I can explain everything," Marianne begged.

He pulled his bristly bar of eyebrows together and stared at her speculatively. Then he glared at the dowager and grumbled under his breath. After studying the crest on the door of the dowager's carriage for a thoughtful moment, he invited them inside the house.

Willow unlocked Marianne's door five minutes later, and she rushed downstairs. She could hear voices from the front parlor and hurried to the door. When she saw Leith so close, she wanted to cry with happiness.

He laughed and scooped her up in his arms and swung her around.

"Enough of that nonsense!" barked the squire, and Leith obeyed, setting Marianne down next to her father. The squire pulled on his coat, and he looked every inch the proud owner of the manor.

"You'd better explain from the beginning," he said ominously. "And it better be a convincing story."

Marianne, in her eagerness to make the truth clear, stammered over her first words, "F-father, it's a-about a stack of love letters." She launched into the story, and the dowager filled in the missing pieces, demanding that the squire keep mum about the part of the letters.

"Leith only deceived the Randomes with his disguise to find the letters, not for any other reason," the dowager added.

"A ramshackle way to go about business," said the squire. "I like a gentleman who acts aboveboard in all matters."

"So do I," said Leith, "but you must understand that I had to approach this matter with stealth, or the blackmailer would not have been revealed. Grandmother was instructed to send the money with a messenger to a certain address in Ashford. It turned out no one lived at the address, but I figured the culprit hailed from Randome's Folly."

The squire rubbed his jaw in thought. "What an imbroglio," he muttered. "Havey-cavey goings-on."

"Well, what would you have done, Mr. Darby, if you were in the same situation?" the dowager asked with some asperity.

The squire glared at Leith. "*I* would not have written

scandalous letters, and most certainly I would not have dressed up like a butler. Your grandson is a regular jester.''

Lady Randome linked her arm to Leith's. ''My grandson is loyal and kind. When I needed his help, he didn't hesitate.'' She gave Marianne a nod. ''Your daughter is a fortunate young woman to have caught my grandson's heart.''

Marianne blushed and glanced at her father. ''I know I went behind your back, Father, but I had no other choice.''

''Hrrmph!'' The squire seemed to mull over what had been said. He eyed Leith from the corner of his eye.

Marianne placed her arm through that of her father and squeezed it. ''Once you told me I could marry a gentleman of my choice, not yours. Well, you forced me to accept Swinton Langley, who, by the way, must be on his way here, but he's not my choice. Leith Sheridan is, and I beg you to accept him.''

The squire started pacing the floor, and Marianne waited tensely for his verdict. Leith's gaze caressed her from across the room, and she knew her choice was right, blessed.

An eager knocking sounded at the front door, then came a flurry of movement. Willow's creaky voice could be heard beyond the closed door of the parlor, then rapid steps. Swinton Langley entered the room, his face unnaturally flushed and his neckcloth askew.

Without issuing a greeting, he launched into impassioned speech. ''They said in the village that a fistfight occurred at this address not an hour ago.'' He took two giant steps toward Marianne. She had never seen him move that fast before. ''Is everything in order?'' His face full of suspicion, Swinton viewed Leith's blood-spattered shirtfront.

When no one answered, he continued, "I have the special license with me. Are we waiting for the vicar to arrive?"

The squire stepped abruptly to the middle of the floor and stared at Swinton. "I regret there won't be a wedding this afternoon, Langley." After giving that announcement, he scrutinized Swinton's face, and Marianne did the same.

Her suitor turned a fiery red, then paled. He took a proprietary hold on Marianne's arm. "I was led to believe that Miss Marianne and I would make a match of it today."

"But you aren't." The squire's clipped response set Swinton's hand atremble.

"But . . . but," he sputtered, "I *must* marry Miss Marianne. You promised me access to her sizable dowry, Squire Darby. Mother and I—"

"I know you need the funds Marianne would bring, but what I want to know is, do you love her?" He stood so close that Swinton took a step back.

"L-love her?" He gave Marianne an uncertain look. "We must get on with the ceremony. If Mother gets wind of this—I have to present her with fait accompli. Otherwise she'll make a heap of trouble for us."

"She abhors the idea of sharing you with anyone, doesn't she?" Marianne asked.

Swinton flinched. "Ah . . . well, I don't think she has any say in the matter."

The squire repeated his question. "Do you, or don't you love Marianne? Give me the truth."

Swinton rubbed his hands in agitation. "I daresay I do."

"You care more about your own welfare," said Leith from the other side of the room.

Swinton didn't reply to that sally.

The squire rocked on his feet. "I believe I shall not give you Marianne's hand, after all, Swinton. Your demeanor shows no warmer feelings toward my daughter." He gave Marianne a censoring glance. "Since she has so foolishly given her love to that young jackanapes"—he indicated Leith with a toss of his head—"I find that she must marry him."

"But our agreement," Swinton said peevishly. "You can't back out now, or I must seek legal help to acquire what you promised." He gave Marianne a glance full of loathing. "Actually I would not want to marry a female who kisses strangers behind trees in full view—"

"It wasn't in full view, Swinton," Marianne said, "you were spying on me."

"Be that as it may. After all, you *are* my fiancée, and no amorous butlers are going to change that fact."

Leith stepped forward. "If it's funds you need, I'm willing to pay the equal of Marianne's dowry to secure her release from a betrothal that was a mistake from the start."

The squire slewed his head around and gave Leith a startled glance. "You would be willing to do that to get my daughter's hand?"

"I would be willing to do more than that. I would gladly give everything I own for her."

"Hmm, well, that's not necessary," the squire said.

Marianne went to Leith and he held her within the safety of his arms.

The squire clapped his hands together. "Swinton, I want you to leave, and *I* shall give you the dowry." He turned to Leith. "As for you, young jester, you shall have

Marianne without a dowry. A bitter pill to swallow, no?''

Leith laughed and swung Marianne around. ''A highly satisfactory solution,'' he said.

''I don't know about that,'' the dowager grumbled, but she didn't pursue the argument.

Swinton took himself off, his step rather buoyant, Marianne thought.

''His mother will be pleased, I think,'' Leith said sotto voce.

Marianne nodded. Her heart melted as she met Leith's loving gaze. In his arms was where she belonged.

''After all this ruckus, I could drink a glass of champagne,'' the dowager said, her voice tender.

The squire muttered something, then went to pull the bellrope. When Willow entered, Darby sent him to fetch a bottle of the best champagne.

The squire stood before Leith and Marianne. ''I take it you want to get married as soon as possible?''

''That's right, Squire Darby,'' Leith said.

''So be it, then.'' Marianne's father seemed to shake himself mentally. He gave Leith a hard punch in the arm. ''Well, Mr. Sheridan, do you like horses?''

Leith laughed and placed a friendly arm around the squire's shoulders. ''Like horses? I'm a member of the Four-in-Hand Club. Let me tell you all about the matched grays I just purchased. . . .''

He led the squire across the room, but over his shoulder he winked at Marianne, and she winked back. Leith would charm his way into her father's heart in no time, just as he had charmed his way into hers.

Nationally bestselling author

JILL MARIE LANDIS

___**COME SPRING** 0-515-10861-8/$4.99
"This is a world-class novel . . . it's fabulous!"
—Bestselling author Linda Lael Miller
She canceled her wedding, longing to explore the wide open West. But nothing could prepare her Bostonian gentility for an adventure that thrust her into the arms of a wild mountain man. . . .

___**JADE** 0-515-10591-0/$4.95
A determined young woman of exotic beauty returned to San Francisco to unveil the secrets behind her father's death. But her bold venture would lead her to recover a family fortune—and discover a perilous love. . . .

___**ROSE** 0-515-10346-2/$4.50
"A gentle romance that will warm your soul."—Heartland Critiques
When Rosa set out from Italy to join her husband in Wyoming, little did she know that fate held heartbreak ahead. Suddenly a woman alone, the challenge seemed as vast as the prairies.

___**SUNFLOWER** 0-515-10659-3/$4.99
"A winning novel!" —Publishers Weekly
Analisa was strong and independent. Caleb had a brutal heritage that challenged every feeling in her heart. Yet their love was as inevitable as the sunrise. . . .

___**WILDFLOWER** 0-515-10102-8/$4.95
"A delight from start to finish!" —Rendezvous
From the great peaks of the West to the lush seclusion of a Caribbean jungle, Dani and Troy discovered the deepest treasures of the heart.